Daniell Comes to Judgement

Daniell Comes to Judgement

New and Vintage Daruwalla

KEKI N. DARUWALLA

NIYOGI
BOOKS

Published by
NIYOGI BOOKS
D-78, Okhla Industrial Area, Phase-I
New Delhi-110 020, INDIA
Tel: 91-11-26816301, 49327000
Fax: 91-11-26810483, 26813830
email: niyogibooks@gmail.com
website: www.niyogibooksindia.com

Editor: Gita Rajan
Cover Design: Misha Oberoi
Layout: Shashi Bhushan Prasad

ISBN: 978-93-85285-59-2
Publication: 2017

Printed at: Niyogi Offset Pvt. Ltd., New Delhi, India

"To the free thinkers of the world".

A story must have bone
a long dreaming Euphrates
of a tail
twitching, incised
by a shiver of illogic.

Moon enough
to allow one one lone frog
to drip endless reverie
on a winter night.

Nerve. Plenty
of nerve.

Arundhathi Subramaniam

CONTENTS

INTRODUCTION

In reading Keki Daruwalla's sensitively written tales about diverse issues and at various locations, I am reminded of Naguib Mahfouz's words: 'The writer interweaves a story with his own doubts, questions, and values. That is art.' And the comparison has a serious intent because a writer's art goes beyond the crafting of a narrative; it embraces social causes and brings a fresh perspective to occurrences that are missed by the ordinary eye. Like Mahfouz, Keki Daruwalla has been in the civil service, and like him too, Keki has spoken up for liberated literary expression. Significantly, the authors have straddled several genres, eager to explore boundaries and cross over them, their narratives showing that the best story is one which disguises its intent, for it captures the reader with the power of telling and permeates the conscience with its tender reflections[1]. Keki Daruwalla, known to most of his admirers as a poet who won the distinguished Commonwealth Poetry Prize for Asia in 1987 and went on become the most easily recognised voice of Indian poetry in English, has taken a fortunate step in bringing

1 Some views reflect my earlier essay on Keki Daruwalla published in *Indian Literature*.

out a selection of his short stories written over several decades. Recently Keki raised a question and provided an answer. 'Poets are turning to the novel. Why? Then again, why on earth not? Fiction presents a cerebral challenge—the plot and how your characters knuckle under or square up to circumstances.' (*The Hindu*, Feb 13, 2016.) Applying this to his own work, one may comment that Daruwalla's high reputation as a poet has often obscured his superb craftsmanship as a writer of short stories. The present collection titled *Daniell Comes to Judgement: New and Vintage Daruwalla* is a much needed volume carrying old favourites along with delightfully new material. The stories dwell in the twilight zone of desires, those that relate to innate passions and reach towards the impossible in search of fulfilment. Such desires are not defined in the ordinary sense of emotional or sexual need but cover a gamut of experiences in India and beyond, in history and contemporary living. The sophisticated and nuanced writing is in control of the form of shorter fiction—a most difficult genre—to render vignettes that will tug at the heartstrings and spark off personal empathies. Like the grand masters of old, for example, Edgar Allan Poe, who said, 'A short story must have a single mood and every sentence must build towards it,' Keki captures the moment and the milieu with exemplary art.

Modern love is only equivalent to a wallet, the author seems to suggest in several stories. Relationships break down, spouses blatantly cheat on each other, young people turn cynical about marriage, and the churning wheel of the economy determines where the heart will be lodged. Urban stress plays on human psychology, morphing it into caricatures of old values such as dignity, affection, and nurturance. The evolution in rural India has stripped away any innocence. But the poet's brush cannot only deal harsh strokes, and

Keki's language mellows to witness nature while emotional devilry plays itself out in society. Within this frame, Daruwalla's short fiction has undergone changes, the older material more realistic and tethered to a plot structure, the recent stories liberated from such expectations and willing to take wing in unknown skies.

In the new stories with which the collection opens, it's gratifying to see Daruwalla writing in the first person as a woman, entering the psyche and contending with themes such as exploitation, mental aberration, jealousy and suchlike. He has always been a gender-sensitive writer but to take the plunge and give narrative voice to a variety of female personae is to risk a creative crossover. The success is spectacular and pertinent to empowerment issues today. 'Daniell Comes to Judgement' echoes the hype over art auctions and the pricing of treasures. Janet, the narrator and custodian of Daniell's precious print, is wary of a dealer who befriends her and offers her a pittance. Though she loses the print in a flood, she regains her confidence through a second chance, a kind of redemption. Another story, 'Garima and a Buried Fragrance', shows how the act of watering a mother's garden, her heritage of womanhood, brings forth the perfumes from buried bulbs, and enriches Garima's day as she greets 'the *poorwaiya* … the east wind … coming like a cone of light at dawn.'

It may be a common assumption that love and betrayal chart parallel tracks but Keki Daruwalla includes unusual woman-centred narratives from his earlier works that are subtle endorsements of feminine strength. 'A House in Ranikhet', 'And on You also be Peace' and 'Crossroads' are among these. Set in different locations and in varying contexts, it's the humanitarian motif of trust that the stories play upon. Women liberated from traditional constraints find their way through challenges that are concomitant with modernity. They will negotiate society with confidence, maybe buy a house, decide on their companions, keep secrets, try strategies of manipulation—and why not? Episodes show the divergences from conventional value systems, with nerve and verve, yet the 'poetic stories,' as Namita Gokhale calls them, carry an astonishing beauty.

A cluster of stories reflect upon identity formations during the national movement. The early favourite, 'Love Across the Salt Desert', speaks of cross-border smuggling and the romance of camel trains. 'The Rann lay like a paralysed monster, its back covered with scab and scar tissue and dried blister-skin.' Young love blossoms amidst danger and despair, and the finale is a triumph of the human spirit over the prejudices of place. As Najab shyly escorts his bride, Fatimah, from the 'alien' land of Pakistan into his paternal home in India, the skies open up with a shower of benediction. Comparable to this is another story, 'When Gandhi Came to Gorakhpur', which is about the call for *swadeshi* and an individual's struggle between profit and sacrifice. Remarkable here is the transformative experience of Shadilal when he meets Gandhi and is reminded of his patriotic promises. To this repertoire is added another story using the political muscle-man, Ram Khilawan, in a haunting tale of forbidden love, 'The Day of the Winter Solstice.'

None of this is polemical. Keki Daruwalla is a consummate storyteller. However, after reading a batch of tales, one is likely to seek the core of the writer's consciousness. Despite Daruwalla's deep interest in Greek and Egyptian history, and in Russia, on which a few stories are based ('Trojan Horse', 'The Hieroglyph Cave', 'A Russian Story'), the core is not in the fascinating plots but in the act of seeking the purpose of human existence. Revisiting mythology helps to interpret the present, and Daruwalla's fine ability to invest the legends with meaning turns the narratives into quest stories of modern day explorers mimicking the old, as if time has rolled over the sands but the hourglass has stood still.

Has human nature evolved or are the elemental passions of love and desire, trust and betrayal, possession and denial still the constitutive segments of the soul? The paradoxes of mortality show up in magnificent stories relating to asceticism, such as 'The Long Night of the Bhikshu,' 'High Pastures' and 'Bird Island.' In a prose piece Keki had written, 'It is not just that the writer has changed his views, his reaction to events, or the way he sees life now as against the way he looked at it earlier … the core problem lies in the writer not being the same man. The bridge with his own past has disappeared.' The bridge can be found; it is made of memories, of images, of dreams—a trope that makes a frequent appearance throughout Keki's work. In Bhikshu's mind, the 'burnt leaf face of his mother flitted through this dream world,' and in a father's quest for his lost son is seen 'an island rise up in front of them, as if some bird god had summoned the entire water fowl kingdom to the skies.' These are intimations of immortality, to recall Wordsworth's phrase, even while they presage mutability and death.

Yet Keki Daruwalla proffers not a dark vision of living but a wise and buoyant one. Politics, humour, caricature, sprightly dialogue, risqué phrases at times, make for the pace of his tales. The characters are recognisable but just beyond our ordinary ken; they speak, act and move, but in a manner that lifts them out of the banal state of our everyday routine.

Keki Daruwalla's stories have received much praise, from critics beginning with Mulk Raj Anand, who placed him among 'the few genuine experimentalists in the new Indian short story.' (*Horizon*) In today's context the stories will no longer be dubbed 'experimental' but I think their genuine merit lies in capturing the social phenomenon of a variously developing India of the last three decades. This includes a recapitulation of significant history and problems of identity, violence, exploitation, love and loss. No single story teller in Indian Writing in English has covered so much ground in so directly engaged a fashion. Coupled with Keki's achievements in novel writing and poetry, this volume of stories speaks for his outstanding achievement as a literary practitioner.

Malashri Lal

Dr Malashri Lal is the Convener, English Advisory Board of the Sahitya Akademi, and Professor of English at the University of Delhi.

DANIELL COMES TO JUDGEMENT

The fog came first, the rains followed and then came the floods—no possibility of getting the sequence wrong. It was damp. And it was cold. There had been nothing like this in the city earlier, not in fifty years. And the waters rose and rose like milk on the boil forgotten on the gas stove. No matter how high you climbed the waters seemed to follow you. There was water everywhere, on the streets, in the houses; the ground floors had been taken over by the floods as if by decree. You couldn't do a thing; even the Communist trade unions were unable to lead a protest march. You couldn't bloody march. The fellows would have had to swim holding wet red flags as they surged forward. Actually, two days before the waters decided to roam our streets, I had through sheer instinct gone down to the cellar, and retrieved three vintage bottles of wine and one of Royal Salute. I firmly believe that anxiety is an inseparable part of a woman's being. Yes the cellar, that's where it all began. And I must lead you by the hand, not only down those rickety wooden steps which sometimes creaked at a heavy footfall, but also take you back two years in time.

His footfall was heavy as I led him down. Why? Was I completely nuts? The light was dim and I had to lead him by the hand, my hand clammy, his dry as winter bark.

'You are not keeping it here, are you, Janet?'

'I am. Why else would I have brought you here?'

'I thought it was for a secret you know what …' And he laughed. Even after his laughter died down, a salacious smile lingered on his lips, epilogue fashion. He looked around at the wine bottles lying in the semi-dark. It was Dad's cellar. He, meaning Dad, loved his wine; pity he didn't finish it all. He never drank anything else, no spirits, vodka, whiskey, bourbon—nothing. Just wine and no other spirit. Everything had to be from the vineyards. I saw him nodding, Mr Vivek Karmarkar, corporate honcho, and so young. He kept gazing at the labels. 'You haven't come here to look at the wines,' I said and laughed. He kept nodding and said nothing. The cellar had got him tongue-tied or what? I wondered. Happens to the corporate rich when they see old houses and a bit of ancient class—sorry for the snobbery. There were three trunks down here, their bottoms resting on a jute mat—Dad didn't want the damp to corrode the trunks. Of course I knew which one had the painting, I mean print. Painting sounds more classy. One had to crouch to open the steel trunk and I noticed the hem of my ankle length skirt trailing the dusty floor. I couldn't see properly, took off my glasses, rubbed them against the sleeve of my top and then inserted the key. The lock clicked open after some effort. I sighed with relief. Why was I getting nervous—alone with a good-looker in the semi-dark. I carefully took the bundle out, the print wrapped securely in muslin. The damp got to me suddenly, the air almost heavy with moisture, and I said to him let's go up. It was he who led me, as we threaded up the winding stairs a bit gingerly, me holding the print in one hand, the other clasped in his. We sat down on the couch, I placed it on my coffee table, leaned back and relaxed.

'Give it air, a painting needs air like good wine when you open a bottle. Even a bit of light won't harm. Shouldn't be exposed to direct sunlight though, not often.'

I unwrapped the print. How was I so uninterested in whatever Dad held dear? A terrible sadness came over me and my eyes watered and he noticed it, Vivek Karmarkar. Dad had a book on the Colonial Painters, am not sure what I did with it. A few artists used to drop by, whether to have a look at me or at Dad's books I can't say, probably both—artists are smooth operators, and I kept them at a distance—yes my coffee and my drinks are yours, but that's about it; yea and I don't much care for hugs; and that arm circling my back I hate with special fervour. Thanks.

'If you're not in the mood, you don't have to show it now. I'll leave, but take a good look at it yourself.' He got up, rather sensitive of the man I must say. I caught him by the arm and made him sit back. I am opening it, I said, and in haste even tore a bit of the fragile moth balled muslin wrap. It, the print I mean, showed a river and three tiered hills, low range after range. The last and the highest range was lit up, the hills in the foreground were shadowed.

'It's the Rope Bridge at Srinagar.'

I spotted it just then, yes there it is I said, putting my finger on it, and he almost slapped my finger away. 'Never touch a painting. Haven't you been to our museums with warnings blazoned all over—"Don't touch."'

'It's a print, not a painting,' I retorted.

The rope bridge started from a brown rock—it had to be brown, isn't it, for the rest of the landscape was blue and green, river and hills. A grey rock wouldn't do. And on the rock was a roofless lookout. At the far bank there was a hint of waves, foam edged, as they slapped against the bank lightly.

'What river could this be in Srinagar? The place is known for lakes.' There are times when almost before the words are out of your mouth, you know you've blundered. I had.

'This is Srinagar Garhwal and the river is Alaknanda, just before it meets the Bhagirathi, to form the Ganga at Devprayag. And the painting is called "The Rope Bridge at Serinagur Garhwal."' He was reclining on the couch, his eyes closed. How does he know that much about Daniell, I wondered.

It was then that I looked down at the caption in gold at the bottom of the print. He was damn right, word for word. He couldn't have seen the caption, the bottom of the print was covered by my elbow.

'It is from Daniell all right.' He didn't have to spell it out. Even I knew that much just by looking at the print. I must get it framed. He nodded. 'You'll need to consult an art restorer. Send it to him or her. I have had one of my paintings de-acidified, didn't even know it needed that sort of treatment. It's a watercolour and was getting wrinkled. I had sent it just for ironing out the wrinkles. She, I mean the art restorer Miss Malhotra, didn't like the expression. You should use the expression "de-wrinkling", she told me. Must say, she reproved me rather gently—you don't snap at a client who is about to shell out money.'

I had an inkling that he was involved in art in a big way. But I suddenly had a wicked thought—trust me. Is he into art because of the women?

We would barge into each other at the club, or at a party thrown by some of the numerous *jagirdars* here, the small nawabs now shorn of their nawabi, still sporting their silver-buttoned brocade achkans and churidars, still embarrassingly polite. Vivek asked me over for a cocktail—first time I had been to his fourth floor apartment. It wasn't a glitzy affair—a decent crowd, not the high and mighty, the best of the whiskey being a Black Label Johnnie Walker. The wine was Jacob's Creek, both red and white. And kakori kababs. That's one snack I remembered. He showed me the de-acidified painting he had talked about, a watercolour by a minor Bengali artist of Nand Lal Bose vintage. It was a landscape, a scabbed ravine sloping down beneath a ruined wall latticed with creepers. An indistinct bird was perched on it, ready to fly off; the painter had managed to get that tension into the bird.

'You need to put a price on that Rope Bridge someday. I'll be there at the sale.'

I restrained a smile. 'Have patience. It is not gonna happen next Friday.' And for good measure I added out of sheer cussedness, 'If it happens at all ...' We both laughed. Laughter can differ; his came out semi-stealthy, one of embarrassment. Mine was a warrior's laugh after you've discomfited a foe.

'You know why I am keen on Daniell? Because I too have an heirloom.'

'What is it?'

'Won't tell.'

He went off to greet a guest who had just come in. I tried to talk to the nobility, sat next to an embroidered silk kurta and churidar, noticed his long waistcord peeping under the hem of his kurta, and restrained a smile—restraint seemed to be the order of the day. *Jagirdars* of the old generation felt a bit uncomfortable in my company. I remembered a chap who asked me at a party once where I was from. And when I told him I was from Goa, he was surprised. 'But you are so fair,' he said.

'Any law against a Goan being fair? We don't have to be chocolate coloured, all of us.' He was very apologetic but had ruined my evening. Later I gave the matter some thought. There could be, why bloody not, some Portuguese blood in me. Forefathers have no role here. One of my foremothers, if I can call her that, could have been laid by a Fidalgo. Who knows, she might have been threatened with the Inquisition in the times of Albuquerque, or whenever the Inquisition got going? Or the fellow may have been plain handsome. Why not the Lord Inquisitor himself?

But I kept thinking of the heirloom Vivek was talking of, and walked over to pester him. He came out with it. Among his father's papers he had come across the will of his great-grandfather. There were papers attached to the will, one of them a news clipping from *The Calcutta Chronicle*. It was an advertisement by William and Thomas Daniell broadcasting their intent to execute twelve paintings of Indian scenes.

I started thinking of the other two trunks. What could be in them? The thought kept nagging me but I put off going down those stairs. Motivation is energy by itself. Mine was near zero. I don't know and don't care if I am making any sense. Then, on a Sunday, I finally did go down, fiddle with the locks, couldn't open the damned things, and came up. That rankled. Couldn't have a restful Sunday siesta. Went down again, and wonder of wonders, the locks clicked open. One trunk had Dad's suits and even his dressing gown. I closed it. The second one had a box of old silver coins, a little over a dozen, some of them old, a few from African countries. It had a bracelet of jade—rectangular pieces on a silver band. Looked lovely. I put it on my wrist. And in the corner of the trunk, again wrapped in muslin was a large cardboard box. I opened it. Dad had written 'Staffordshire' on the box. Lovely ceramic with a painting on it looking like something out of William or Thomas Daniell. I had read up on them now. The two, fine artists both, sailed for India from Gravesend on 7 April 1785, arriving in Calcutta the next year via China. And of course Vivek had told me that Thomas had been permitted by East India Company to come as an engraver. The first twelve plates were executed in etching and aquatint. The colouring was done by local painters who must have been paid in copper. Then they toured the country and even went to Madras, a year after the defeat of Tipu Sultan.

I kept the dish back in the trunk. These items had lain in the cellar, safely, for almost a decade. Why expose them to the hurly burly of the world and the market? I rummaged through the trunk again, my hands acting as eyes. My hand encountered a small hard object. It was a pistol, with a small pouch containing ammo. You kept a pistol, Dad! We never ever knew. After a fortnight, when Vivek chanced upon me, I told him of the ceramic find, but skipped the details.

'The trouble with you is I can't bring you a bottle of wine, because you have a better stock than I can dream of. But yes, I will drop in for a cup of coffee one day.' And he dropped in with a lovely Patola saree. The stairs were still dim lit. I was cursing myself, why couldn't I get a brighter bulb put in. His footfall wasn't as heavy this time, was he treading on tiptoe? I looked down and found he was in his socks, I never noticed him take off his shoes. As I bent to insert the key in the lock, I stumbled, and he caught me by the waist, turned me around and kissed me. A long lingering kiss it was and I didn't push him away. I suppose such things happen. To make things clear I drew back, opened the trunk and took out the box, containing the Staffordshire earthenware dish. We went up and I took it out proudly and admired it in the light. We held that lovely dish together.

'That is the painting of the ruins of Ferozshah Kotla. It has been so beautifully reproduced on the dish. 1795, I should suppose.'

Thomas Daniell had taken care to foreground the painting with a human scene, a turbaned man with a stave, his wife a few steps behind him, like all good Indian wives, and a buffalo in front, like all good buffaloes. (The buffaloes are up in arms these days because of all the attention being paid to the cows, but that is incidental. The Buffalo Union is, according to the latest reports, protesting over the fact that their *Bhainsshala* is not being given the kind of respect that a *Gaushala* gets).The Kotla or the Daniell ruins displayed walls with plaster peeling off and the naked weather-beaten bricks visible. But a hot kiln and ceramics can make even erosion gleam.

'You're not showing much interest in this dish, are you?'

'I have other interests at the moment,' and he shifted in his seat to face me—we were both sitting on the couch—and grabbed me by the waist. I didn't resist, I don't remember if I was falling for him or it was the moment. Moments carry their own destiny with them, especially in matters of love. Or did I use the wrong word? Lust?

'Be careful, I am a virgin.'

He nodded, took out his wallet and pulled out a condom. The so-and-so had come prepared! Self-assured bastard, he knew, knew all the time that he could get away with it! But he was very careful.

Obviously such matters don't end with the inaugural. There have to be sequels to Bismillah and Shri Ganesh. Then one day at the Coffee House where my friend Roopa and I met regularly on Mondays, she said apropos of nothing, you know a bit about Vivek, don't you?

'I don't get you, Roopa. What are you trying to say?'

'You know what I am trying to say.'

I shook my head, opaque me, not so opaque, stubborn mule rather.

'Let's say, if there is a University for adultery, Vivek Karmarkar would be the Vice Chancellor.'

'Sorry, I got distracted. Didn't hear you.'

'You did,' and she got up. We had already paid. I couldn't tell her that we were both single, adultery didn't get onto the picture edgewise.

Roopa's poniard had its effect. I stopped it, meaning I gave him the brush off. 'Why?' he asked. 'Because,' I replied—a mono syllable countered with two.

Earlier we had been sparring over the price jocularly, as if it was a charade, which we both knew, it was not. Then, after the break-up, if one could call it that—why does language attempt to define every wayward wind that moves through a relationship—he telephoned. 'Morning, Janet, this is business we are talking of. I have a firm offer.'

'For?' I can be brutal. But wasn't it a legit question? What if he was offering matrimony?

'The print, Janet. A lakh.'

'Are we talking dollars?'

'No. Rupees, damn it. It is just a print, not a canvas, for God's sake.'

'Forget it, Vivek. This is an original print, from the first batch, *virgin*.' I just wanted to see how he'd counter that. Would *virgin* trigger some nasty riposte? Would he say, 'Something that you can't say for yourself anymore?' No, he didn't.

'You are missing a very good deal, Janet. Think it over. A lakh is not something to be sneezed at. You will regret it, I tell you, you'll be sorry!'

He had a point. A lakh was a lot of money in the early seventies.

The rain never stopped and the waters kept rising. The radio repeated warnings of the Dam being in danger. Water was being released in torrents, and the villages downstream were in a spin. Boats were commandeered for rescue. The day was dark with an overhang of a huge black cloud that refused to budge. The forecasts from the Met Office were gloomier than the skies. What would happen to the print, that became my chief anxiety. Vivek had told me that the painting of the Srinagar Rope Bridge had never been signed. Trust the fellow to say that, just to bring down the price, I thought. How did he know? Dogged bugger, normally saw to it that he got what he wanted. I decided to leave it with Vivek. Nothing could possibly happen to his apartment. I would also get a glimpse of the Dam, right behind. But I dithered. Who doesn't? It already seemed too late. The waters were climbing up the steps that led to the verandah of my house. The road was still navigable, thank God, the waters rushing down into the drains. The radio said there had been incidents of looting. A calamity is always a godsend to some of my countrymen. A warehouse catches fire, loot the blessed place before everything inside burns down. It's a national service you are doing, guys!

As I went down to get the print, I thought of the pistol also. What if someone robbed me? Tucked it in my purse.

Some autos were plying. I hailed one, screamed, folded my hands and he came, out of compassion I think.

The elevator hissed to a stop at his floor. He saw the newspaper-wrapped piece (shame on me) tucked under my armpit and guessed what it was.

'So Janet, one gets to see you at last.' Smile big enough to drive a truck into. 'Come and sit here on the couch with me. You are not comfy on that chair.'

'I am very happy here.'

'What will you have, Darling?'

'Don't bloody darling me, Vivek. This is business, you know you said that over the phone once!'

'Hasn't it always been business between us, Luv!'

I noticed he was leering. He came over to where I was sitting and put his arm around me. I shrugged him off, but gently. 'Vivek—two propositions, I...'

'Luv, I thought it was my job to proposition you! You don't have to!' He threw his arms around me and started kissing.

I shove him back to his settee a good six feet away—can't stand him near me. 'Listen, Vivek. Can you keep the print safe, till the flood waters go down?'

'No.'

His expression reminded me of rust on scrap iron.

'You mean it, don't you?'

'Yes,' he answered, his eyes two metal discs. 'You are helpless, Janet. Why should I bail you out? You could climb on to your rooftop, and sit the night out with your damn print under an umbrella.'

'You offered a lakh for this once. Take it.'

'Ten thousand.'

'What!'

'You heard me right, not a rupee more. You could have got a lakh. Told you you'd regret it, spurning me. Things could change if you stay the night. Where can you go? You are helpless, Luv.'

His arms held wide, he advances towards me; easy prey, hare caught in headlights, that's what you think. Don't you dare come near! I pull out the pistol, my purse trembles, or is it the hands? He just laughs, disbelievingly.

I am no laughing matter, Vivek. Point my pistol at the ceiling and fire (wish I had aimed at him), notice the plaster coming down like debris heralding a landslide in the hills.

'Not so helpless,' I shout, my voice drowned by the gunshot echo running around the room, rush out, down the steps, no time to wait for the hissing elevator, hear footsteps behind. He is hurrying after me, shouting, 'I'm sorry, Janet, was just teasing you, it was a joke …' blah blah blah blah.

It is a different street now. The Dam has broken, the waters are a torrent, a river in spate; boats are plying on the street, see an army boat with an officer cautioning, 'Stay put'; Vivek following, screaming, 'Stop, Janet, didn't mean what I said.' Making amends, is he, a bit late in the day!? I wade through the waters. A wave, that's what I'd call it, knocks the print out of my hand. The army guy catches me before I go under. Vivek doesn't have the same luck; he and the Daniell are swept away by the flood waters.

The rest is a blur, but I do remember we could have removed the bulbs from the lamp posts, we were that high sitting in the boat, at least fifteen feet off the ground. I believe they put trucks piled with sandbags to fill the breach, and at least one truck got swept away like Vivek and the Daniell.

When the waters recede a week later, I go with Roopa and two of her servants to my house. There is no electricity. The cellar is still under water, wine bottles floating, everything ruined, clothes, carpets, timber; am afraid of stepping into the water in the cellar, what if one got electrocuted. Roopa's domestics bring gumboots from somewhere. I go down, see something floating—it is Daniell's ceramic dish with the ruins of Ferozshah Kotla painted on it. 1795, he had said. Some of my depression vanishes.

☛

Five years later.

I get a call from London.

'Miss Janet Fernandez, I am speaking on behalf of Sotheby Auctioneers. We believe you have the Staffordshire ceramic dish with Thomas Daniell's painting. Would you like to put it up for auction, Ma'am?'

'How did you know I had it?'

'We get to hear these things. It's our job.'

'How much will it fetch?'

'The base price we're fixing is twenty thousand pounds sterling …'

GARIMA AND A BURIED FRAGRANCE

I wake up at four in the morning. Bad time to go to the loo. When you come back to bed you discover sleep has deserted you. Father, decent old man, fond of me though he could never bring himself to show any trace of affection, used to call sleep the land of nod, linguistic crumbs from the Victorian table. He was proud of such phrases and my sister Gauri and I would be hard put to restrain our smiles. I toss on the bed but can't get anywhere near sleep; switch on the light and try reading a story by an Icelandic writer, fail; mind keeps wandering, minds love travel. I think of Mother—paralysed hip down a year before she died. Her mind must have been nomadic, far-roving mind visiting old places, even those never seen, while the legs remained stilted, stalled, torpid.

Can't go on with the Iceland story because the mind is at its tricks. I reflect on the volcanic ash over the skies of Europe, paralysing every airport in the continent, making Vishwanathan Anand take a cab and drive what must have been a thousand kilometres (it took him forty hours) to be at Sofia to defend his World Chess Championship. What would an Indian movie make of this dramatic event? Aamir Khan as Anand, racing on a Yamaha through gorgeous scenery—Rhine forest, Alps (goodbye geography and road maps) with the German police after him for speeding, landing at Sofia, covered with dust, two day stubble on unwashed chin, and sitting down against Vaselin Topalov and besting him. Salaam, Bollywood. But the film is a flop. You can't possibly have an affair in a World Chess Championship. The script writer can't conjure up a believable scene—Bishop making advances to the Queen, why not? Film fails at Box Office same time as Anand loses to Magnus Carlson. Newspaper headlines called it 'double whammy.'

Weeds in my garden, Mother's rather, not much of a garden, but it is the small lawn I am bothered about, weed-choked, have been telling the mali to burn the grass. Moving into Mother's little house is a blessing; there's work to do, as in any new place you move into; and it has kept my mind occupied for the past two months. If the mind is engaged things like regret and pointless rumination need an entry pass they are not likely to get.

I seem to breathe acrid smoke; it is coming through the window. What could be burning? Couldn't be the leaves set aflame by the mali—no one would do that at four! The bell rings. Who could be ringing the bell at four, damn it? I look at the clock, which says five. Iceland has taken away an hour of my life, Iceland and Vishwanathan Anand and a volcanic ash cloud. I take a deep breath—not the right thing to do when there's smoke around. The house on fire, or what? Is it the chowkidar ringing to say the car door is open or telling me the house is on fire? I recall I don't have a car anymore. If you don't have a car, your car door can't be open—I should have taken logic for my masters. I walk to the door, undo the latch but don't open the door, draw the window curtain aside and peep through the adjacent window, notice a cycle rickshaw there. Who could it be? It is Mausi, my mother's elder sister. Can't believe it. We hug. She pays off the rickshaw guy, I take her suitcase in, and we hug again. And then, cross as ever, she asks, '*Kya hua,* Garima? Have been ringing the bell for ten minutes! You sleep like Kumbha Karna.' I am not into the inlets and interstices of the *Mahabharata*—oh sorry, this here is the *Ramayana*. Me and Kumbha Karna, me slim, after seventeen years of married life and that pot bellied glutton K.K.! Dad was keener on our entry into the *Iliad* rather than our own epics. But K.K. was someone I recalled. He beat up Indra, that Head Master of godlings. Dad had all those nineteenth-century verse translations of books 'from the East.' I recalled two lines:

> And he to save the suffering world
> His bolt at Kumbha Karna hurled.

Nothing came of it and Indra and his bolt (was it a thunderbolt?) got beaten up by K.K. I nurse some sympathy for the fellow. I am an Aquarian and our symbol is Kumbha, the pot. After years of penance and prayer to the supreme, he was at last given an audience with Brahma, as these congress types are given an audience with Rahul Gandhi. As the devotee is asking a boon, Indrasana, Indra's throne, Saraswati at the behest of Indra, makes him tongue-tied, twists his tongue to such an extent that the poor blighter asks for Nidrasana, a bed for sleeping. Trust these Brahmins, who had a monopoly on Sanskrit—others would be burnt alive if they ventured anywhere near the language—to come up with such a story.

Now how does one tell Mausi all this? One doesn't. She tells me even before she has stepped into her yet-to-be-prepared room, 'I'll be gone by *navratra*. You must still be a heathen, eating pork even during those nine sacred days.' And mutton, I add wickedly, but now we call it lamb, Mausi. I get a cold stare. Ungrateful me. I sense why she has come. Just to be with me, recent divorcee. 'Recent divorcees' need sympathy. It's only when divorcees turn old and remain unhitched, that old ladies start looking hard at their bellies and speculating, 'Is she pregnant? If so, who's she sleeping with?'

I never eat pork. Where did she get the idea? I suppose it is the language. If you say, as she has just done, '*Thu tho navratra mein bhi suwar khaati hogy*!' it sounds nasty enough, the kind of a putdown well delivered and well deserved at the other end. Pretty bitchy of me to think the way I am thinking now. Instead I ask her, 'You could have phoned Mausi, I'd have come in a cab and picked you up.' No answer. 'And there are cabs at the station, you could have taken them. A rickshaw at night!'

'Morning.'

'But it must have been dark when you left the station. Dangerous.'

'Read the papers. It is your cab drivers who commit murders and rape their passengers, never these rustic rickshaw drivers.'

I don't argue. There are times you can't; even if you can it is pointless. A believer in bucolic bliss, my aunt. I change the sheets in her room, switch on the geyser, and get some tea ready, the cardamom tea cooked on the *choola* with milk and sugar added, just as she likes. The paper comes hurtling in, rolled inside a rubber band. One day the fellow is going to shatter the window glass. Mausi says nothing though she looks at me pointedly. I don't react. She sees the front page and exclaims, 'Oh so now he has gone to Arabia, has he? *Aur koi jageh nahin mili*?'

I have to draw the line somewhere or I'll never hear the end of it. 'Mausi, enough! You know my feelings. Not a word against him!'

'Arre, what have I said! All I want to ask is has he gone there for Haj? Is he doing Umra? Harmless questions you ask of anyone who goes to Arabia.'

Angry as I am I almost smile. A put-downer is necessary. 'And it is not Arabia. It is Saudi Arabia. Arabia exists only in English translations of *Thousand and One Nights*, Mausi.'

'Yes, yes. It is named after a dynasty, the Saudi one, just as some of our chamchas wanted to turn our country into Indira's India. But it will revert to Arabia one day, just as the USSR reverted to Russia.'

My aunt has more sense than me. Her tongue is a rebel, though. 'I was just wondering about his next jaunt. Rwanda? No, but he could go to Kenya where they are slaughtering elephants. This party has great respect for animals—if you shoot a mad dog you'd be in jail. And if you trade in cattle you might as well be dead.' I ignore her absurd comments, no point entering into a fight the very first day.

I smell smoke, again; migrant farmers, tractor-owning ones, are burning the stubble from the paddy fields. It is that acrid smoke descending on us. I remember shouting at my mali a good two months back, in fact a day after I landed here. The lawn was plagued with weeds. Burn the thing, I had said. Remembered I also had been weeded out. That had lent some passion to my decision. He wasn't convinced. He had dug up the place a bit, got rid of the weeds by the roots and discovered bulbs in the ground.

The doorbell rings and my domestic Indu comes in, and seeing Mausi, touches her feet. Small-town courtesies, it wouldn't happen in cities. Good lady, Indu I mean. I am relieved, don't want another minute with aunt alone, or she would home in on the divorce. Even if you love a niece, and she does love me, it is the juiciness of a divorce that attracts people. What went wrong, and then an unasked question hovers in the background always, did it have anything to do with the bedroom? Was he turning impotent, some item not as rock hard as it used to be? No one dare ask that, but you can see it in their eyes.

And let's admit it, it's one subject you can only talk to your mother about. No one else; quietly over days lying beside her late into the night, in quiet almost muffled tones, the words spilling out from your insides, loaded with feeling and regret and at times grief, for there has to be a bit of grief, isn't it, leaving someone or getting nudged out by circumstances or the cussedness of law or another woman. Only Mum could be the one I could say all this to. She could almost echo my feelings. Are daughters echoes of mothers, or is it the other way around? And Mum is dead. How do you tell the whole story, the unravelling of the entire *dastan* to her sister? You'd need a hundred and one nights. Everything suddenly started irritating him. How come? He was fighting in the office—news does filter back somehow. What has happened, I ask. 'Don't ever talk to me about office! Wasn't that our understanding right at the start?'

'Yes it was, but now things are hotting up I hear.'

'Shut up! Shut up I say!'

He'd never been like that, never spoke half as rudely. What has come over him, I start wondering. Then I hear that Sudipta, who was in HRD in the office has been thrown out. I still can't put two and two together. Wives of colleagues enter with serious faces. When husbands gallivant, friends start wearing masks with lines of worry, suits everyone, friends, wife and the occasion. Once I even told them if he has a fling I am not bothered, as long as he doesn't fall in love with her. What are you saying, asked one of them. What do you think love is, some well in which you fall? Another added, it is the bed where love splashes, don't forget.

Then he told me he was leaving office, had got a better offer. What better offer, they've thrown you out, is it? He almost turned violent. They threw Sudipta out as well, I added for good measure. Once they threw her out you couldn't take it anymore. All this fever and fret and fighting because you couldn't get your hands on her again, isn't it? Poor you! He became apoplectic. Caught my arms and shook me. That was it. In the court room the judge asked me if we had any children. I shook my head and he nodded. Oh, a barren woman, *baanj* as we call her in our dulcet butter-wouldn't-melt-in-its-mouth Hindustani. Poor chap, what else could he do but throw her out. That's what that male judge's nod was all about. Thank you judge for being so understanding.

After all I had my mother's little house with the little lawn, nestling in a small town, a half hour's drive to Lucknow. Six months back I had come and planted jasmine vines and engaged the mali. Now after the break-up I decided to move here, in the suburbs where jackals used to howl at night when I was a kid. An acquaintance from the town, Dipti, sent me bulbs, a cut from a night-flowering vine, herbs, summer hyacinth. Your mother left them with me, she said, as she stood by and helped me with planting them. It has been over two months now.

Mausi never has breakfast. Her lunch is getting ready, buttermilk being churned in the kitchen without my saying a word to Indu. Carrots and peas are being diced. A bite won't do me any harm, and I nibble at the paratha. But Indu is from Gorakhpur, and she calls it *parathi*. You cross a district border and the language turns; small tributaries of dialect fork out, a slurring of vowels you didn't notice earlier, a softening of consonants. It is not just the language, even genders change. Ah well.

☛

Clouds. I hear distant thunder a skyline away. Dusk is the time the mali waters the lawn and he is at it. I am proved wrong. Of a sudden I smell something good, the wind has brought it through the window, as it brings bird cries. What could it be, this fragrance which reminds me of old days somehow? It is the first time the garden has given off its fragrance, its *mehak*, as the mali calls it. The bulbs have come alive. The *poorwaiya*, the east wind, is cool and moist and welcome, arriving like a cone of light at dawn, heavy with the scents from the garden and the bulbs Mother had left behind, some of them in the ground, and Dipti's flowering shrubs. I thought the frangipani shrub had died. It seems to have revived. Forgotten flower beds, buried bulbs reminding you they are not done. Each flower has a different and a definitive scent, but language hasn't managed to give each *one* a name.

A wistful fragrance floods my senses in spasms. What would have happened if I had got the lawn burnt in my anger? Would the smells have wafted up to where I was, next to the window? The mind wanders. What if a songbird is put in a tandoor? Would she of a sudden start singing? Get rid of your bleak images, I tell myself.

I am in a state of semi-sleep now and the dream-boat embarks—I think of incense trees, the ones sent by the King of Punt to Queen Hatshepsut of Egypt in a boat—he had no clear idea what exactly she had asked for; she wanted vines of some sweet smelling saplings. He sends off a whole frankincense tree, in fact a grove of trees. That's how kings respond. An Incense Fleet moving out from myrrh terraces, loaded with resin and frankincense, ivory and gold, hugging the shores of the Red Sea as it sails towards the throne of the two lands, Upper and Lower Egypt. Now of course they were linking Queen Hatshepsut with Sheba. 'The best of myrrh is upon her limbs, her fragrance is divine dew.' The incense tree, however, is engraved in the Egyptian's temple to Goddess Hathor. Historians are now confused between the two. Punt, Hathor, Hatshepsut, Sheba crowd my brain as I doze off.

GOD'S OWN COUNTRY

The doorbell rings. It is bloody three in the afternoon. Must be some hulking male. Women have more sense than barging in at this hour. It's summer for Chrissake! I was right and I was wrong. There are three hulks.

Are you gentlemen from Haryana?

Yes Madam, how did you guess?

Just.

Be enigmatic, keep people guessing, puts males on the defensive. They came straight to the point though, in fact the speaker introduced himself as Devindar Mohan. Madam, this is a big project, a prize of a hundred million dollars has been announced.

By whom exactly? We start fencing now, playfully. *By a Millionaire Madam.* Oh so he is taking *vanaprastha*, leaving all his money to charity? *He has hundreds of millions Madam, in dollars.* Which forest is he getting into? *Madam is joking.* No, no I mean it—with forests thinning away, what with timber-felling, things are tough. But the plus point Mr Mohan and flunkies is that tigers too are thinning away. So he will be safe. The bad news is he may not find a rishi easily these days—it is only a few rapist sadhus who are now to be found in forests, hiding from the police, or possibly a runaway *sadhvi* involved in placing a bomb somewhere. No, no, kindly don't interrupt, I am not sure where the rishis could have disappeared. They could be in cities, coaching the branches of some vast tree trunk of an organisation, or they could have migrated en masse to Nagpur, don't you think? Or shall we say, the tigers before they migrated (couldn't have been to Nagpur, there's drought there) to more wooded habitats, could have eaten up the rishis. *No, no Madam, how can that be? Tigers have sixth sense—they wouldn't attack rishis or sadhvis.* Nor does the NIA, I answer. You never know Mr Dev Mohan. Sadhu or *sadhvi* flesh or a criminal's may be tasting the same to the tiger, spirituality doesn't have a taste, *zaika*, as we say in Urdu, no particular tactile intimations which could deter the jungle cats. (At times it feels nice to be pedantic).

I even make a foray, not very successfully, into rhyme. To the lion and the boar/the sadhvi and the whore/taste similar. The last line is a letdown; I search for a rhyme—soar, score, more, four, pour, lore—nothing fits. Sad. But please go on Mr Dev, you don't mind me calling you Dev, I hope. That Devindar could twist my jaw. Imagine, you mouth a name and the jaw gets askew and you have to run to the dentist. Will you have some tea? They decline. I feel relieved, my help only arrives after six in the evening and by then I should be out of the house. She, meaning the help, lets out the pigeons from their coop on the terrace. I ask them what the prize is all about. We already told you, they reply, to find the gentlest person on earth.

Why have you come to me? And who is your sponsor?

We can't tell you the name. It is secret.

Let me guess, it is a Non Resident Indian?

Right Madam, you are on the ball.

And he is a Gujarati.

Very right! How did you guess?

All NRI's are from Gujarat. (Loud laughter) Someone from Bharuch or Bulsar or Bardoli? Now I believe Bulsar has been turned to Valsad.

And Bharuch to Broach madam.

When is Delhi going to be called Indraprastha Mr Dev?

Hope they do it fast.

Shubh shubh bolo Mr Dev. But they will have to find two names, Prachin Indraprastha for Old Delhi and will it be Navin Indraprastha for New Delhi? Wouldn't know madam, Hindi genders are confusing. Do they mean Hindi engenders confusion? I don't ask them.

I now pop a sedative into my mouth, time to be serious, summon my recently-lost gravitas and get down to business. I hope this would be over fast because I am scheduled to command a flight in the evening. A jaguar flight is no walk in the park. Dev comes to the point fast. This project has got airborne now. We want to find out the gentlest person on the planet. The sponsor plans to have a great function. It will be on the same scale as a Miss Universe contest, with twelve men or women on the stage. The selection process is really stringent. They will be asked questions. I immediately interrupt.

Let me make a guess. Madam or Sir, no let's put the question to a lady, what will you do with the money? And she'll say (I affect an accent and my voice turns squeaky) Oh I will give three fourths of it to a leprosarium. And what about the one fourth you still have in your bank? That's twenty five million dollars isn't it? I again affect an accent, Oh that, or shall we say most of it, I'll give to the Blind School on the Lodhi Road. The applause will be deafening. But please go on.

You will also be on stage madam.

Me, why on earth?

You look after pigeons. Your other acts of gentleness are well known. But we have principally come to you for your recommendations.

Recommendations?

Yes, whom would *you* recommend?

For what?

To be acknowledged as the gentlest person on the planet. We have been on the subject for the last twenty minutes, haven't we?

Fellow is getting aggressive, I notice.

Why not Mr Khattar, the Haryana Chief Minister? He was so gentle with the Jats during their agitation. They wanted to be included in the reserved category, remember? Imagine what would have happened if the police had started firing on the mobs, as they burnt and pillaged? A hundred could have died. Actually the entire state and the Haryana Police deserve to be commended for their gentleness. But then you can't give the award to the state, can you?

We can't Madam.

I notice they were uncomfortable with my suggestion. We were even thinking of Ramdevji as one of the contestants, but then he made that statement about cutting off the heads of all those who refused to shout '*Bharat Mata ki jai*.' That made it difficult.

Yes Devji, even if these are hypothetical heads of hypothetical national heretics, he can't make it this year. St. Francis of Assisi wouldn't approve.

Madam, the judges will be from either Gujarat or Nagpur. We are not inviting any Christian, I mean western judges, and certainly none from Italy. We would have you know that a Mediterranean chapter has also been opened at Casablanca to find out the gentlest persons there. And we'll start another chapter headquartered in Ecuador the moment the debris from the earthquake is cleared. That will be our South American chapter. And Madam you will be both compere and contestant.

That's not possible, I say. Madam everything is possible if you are a NRI from Gujarat these days. With that parting shot they take their leave.

☛

Good God, it is five already? I am piloting a jaguar—is it to Halwara or is it a fly by on the border—keep the Pakistanis a bit worried. The Air Chief likes that sort of thing, the Pakistani pilots scrambling to their fighters and waiting for the radar to tell them whether I've crossed the border or not. I hurriedly put on my uniform, thank God the pick-up car is there. We drive to Hindon. 'Speed up damn it,' I shout at the driver. These drivers in uniform don't like being shouted at by women, even by a Wing Commander. Fortunately at the air base I am saluted all the way till I get into my jaguar. An Air Commodore is taking a lift with us, Madam, says my Assistant. They come for weekends to Delhi—miss their wives, and he snickers. Don't like him being cheeky and snub him. His papers are in order, I hope. Haven't checked them, he answers—phone from Air Headquarters, Ma'am. He knows my temper, but I let that pass. No point taking up cudgels with Vayu Bhavan. It should have been called Vayu Sena Bhavan, but trust these CPWD guys to stumble. I haven't greeted the Air Commodore as I should have, wouldn't have cost me anything. I curse myself and take off.

Within minutes the Air Commodore walks into the cockpit! I can't believe it. 'Good evening, Sir, but no one walks into my cockpit without my permission and I never give permission.' I can be damn abrupt I can tell you.

'You need not break sweat. Permission won't be necessary Wing Commander,' he says with an affected accent, and he draws out a pistol—a Beretta. I am not easily zapped, mind you. 'We take off for Lahore and land there and nothing is gonna happen to you, get me Lady. But one false move and I blow your brains out. And I have a bomb belt around my chest.' He shows me the bomb belt and the bomb, a square or rather rectangular slab. I am impressed though I am damned if I am going to show it.

'I will do whatever you ask me to, Sir.'

'Don't sir me, I am not what you and your bum of an assistant think I am. I am Jehadi Jamaluddin of Jaish-e-Muhammad. Do as I say and you won't regret it.'

Won't regret it! First woman Wing Commander of the Air force, and her plane, that too a Jaguar, gets hijacked! Over my dead body Chum.

'Won't you sit down, Jehadi Jamal,' I say pointing to the only seat in the cockpit.

We keep flying for the next twenty minutes or is it half an hour, Jehadi Jamal and I. We are overflying Lahore Air Commodore, I mean Jehadi Jamal, please strap yourself and take that seat. He isn't aware of my plan. Is that Lahore? he asks. Of course it is, I answer. Actually we are overflying Gurgaon, but thanks to the pollution he can only see a jungle of concrete slathered with a mist that is half poison and half haze. I dive now and warn the jehadi, 'Strap yourself or you'll get hurt!' He can hardly keep his balance, takes my advice and straps himself on the seat. My plan has succeeded. I come out of the dive and fly up almost perpendicularly and the jehadi throws up. Got him where I wanted.

As we touch an elevation of twenty thousand feet I press the seat pedal. I have seated the bugger on the ejection seat. It is a lovely sight, his face as he flies out of the plane into thin air. That's the way to deal with jehadis. I pump my fist, circle slowly as I lose height and land at Hindon.

☛

It is seven and they come back at seven. Husbands. Mine comes back tired usually, and I give him a cup of tea, naturally. I watch him bouncing up the steps. I let him ring the bell and shuffle around the landing. I open the door. One look at me and the smile disappears from his lips and the fatigue of centuries descends into his eyes. A bolt of sympathy for him, that's what I suddenly feel. Poor guy, he is handcuffed to me. Matrimony can be wearing. One look at me and my avocado coloured face, and the pulse of light has gone out from his eyes. It is not the colour of my face that bothers him, it is the expression squatting there that is his worry. 'Did you remember to take the tablet?' he asks. Now how do I tell him that I get confused between the SSRI's and the SNRI's, between Luvox and Cymbalta. These anti-depressant drugs are a murky ocean in themselves.

THE ARREST

I was at her place when they came to arrest him.

Three Inspectors in one car and a Deputy Commissioner, looking very serious, alone in another. Big team, I thought, to get just one man, and one who was not running. The sirens blared spasmodically, more to keep the crowd from getting in the way. The three got out of their huddle and scrambled to open the door of the big officer's car, a Toyota SUV. The TV crews waited in the sun.

As I said earlier, I was at Kokila's place when they came to arrest her husband, had been with her since I heard the news. It was the least I could do for an old friend. I avoided questions. What can you ask a wife whose husband has shot someone? She said absolutely nothing apart from the first hug and 'Thank you, Aarti, for coming. Never needed you more.' Yes and she asked me if I would have a cup of tea. After that she clammed up. Maybe an hour later or less, she of a sudden whispered, 'When he came back he said, "there's nothing to talk about, Kokila."' Then a while later she said, 'It wouldn't have happened but for that yellow journal and the rubbish that spilled out.'

It wasn't actually rubbish, though certainly malicious. The pervasive malice of the media has to be seen to be believed. How they love to rub your nose in the dirt.

'What's he doing?'

'Just lying down, asked not to be disturbed.'

His brain must be awhirl with God knows what thoughts. Last lie-down on a decent bed.

They had been friends, Brij Bhushan and Shekhar. Such things happen between friends. Why she fell for Shekhar, one doesn't really know. It was not a question of wine and roses. It started with tennis. Brij didn't play. Kokila did. Shekhar was good at it, especially that first serve of his, which daunted most players except Kokila. They played mixed doubles on the gravel courts in the morning, with tea and toast to follow. On Sundays an omelette was also thrown in. Gossip, bitching about colleagues and politicians and the world in general, was of course an essential part of the breakfast at the Delhi Gymkhana. Nothing happened, as far as I gather, during the first few years. It was when they shifted to the lawn courts in the evening that brought them closer. From the bath in the changing rooms to the Bar, a martini with an olive thrown in and layered with crushed ice, a glass of red wine, on Saturdays even a gin and tonic.

People started giving knowing looks. That's even worse than whispered gossip. People are too civilised, by which I mean cautious, to slip in an innuendo early on. Whispers become louder. Then sometime or the other, some place or the other one blunders. Or chance moves in. Who was it who wrote about 'a sigh too deep and a kiss too long/ and then comes a mist and a weeping rain/ but life is never the same again.' Well for Brij and Kokila, life would never be the same again.

I hardly dared to say anything to Kokila. Even if you are the best of friends—we went back a long way, actually from school—you just can't touch on such delicate issues. One wrong word (and words can never be 'right' in matters such as these), and you could lose a friend for life. Suppose she doesn't react harshly but just tells me, 'Easy Aarti, easy,' I would never know how to look her in the eye again.

The first time I suspected something—a woman's intuition it was—was when I saw her and Shekhar coming out of the Mandarin at the Taj Mansingh. I never go to the Mandarin or Bukhara or even the Coffee Shop at the Taj. They are beyond me, a Professor of Chinese at the School of Foreign Languages, but my Uncle was here from Mumbai and he had taken me there. They got into different cars but I noticed a glow on Kokila's face I hadn't seen before. This must be love I thought, happy for Kokila. She confirmed my suspicions one day with a seemingly throwaway line. 'I am looking for a small quiet place Aarti, away from noise, have you anything in mind?' I shook my head. Thank God I didn't question her—what exactly are you looking for? What a shambles it would have been. And one day she confided in me, after I had told her casually to be careful.

'What do you mean, Aarti?'

'People are talking. Just be careful.'

'You won't open up, will you?'

'Playing poker, that's what you're up to, with everything to lose, Kokila. Be careful, that's all I said.'

'Can't be careful, Aarti, I am besotted.'

And then this. Brij went with a pistol to Shekhar's office. Why Shekhar was there at the office I wouldn't know. It was Sunday, dash it. What happened there also I wouldn't know. But Brij shot his wife's lover AND, you won't believe this, dropped his card at the table and walked away. That's what the peon, the only witness, was telling all the channels about, the card flung on the table with a rather disdainful flick of the hand. This was two or maybe three hours ago.

Brij came out the moment he heard the police cars. Kokila started crying. The Deputy Commissioner said in a tone that would have done credit to a James Hadley Chase novel, 'Mr Brij Bhushan Nigam, we are arresting you for murder. Anything you say...'

'I am not going to say a thing, so you can spare me the speech, Sir. Won't be necessary. I am sure you have a warrant.'

Deputy Commissioners don't like being interrupted. 'Not necessary in these circumstances.'

Brij did not react. An Inspector gestured towards a pair of handcuffs he was holding, but the DC shook his head. Brij walked with them and got into the car. His two domestics looked at the whole scene, not believing what they saw, their mouths agape. Kokila was sobbing away. The police cars grated through the gravel leaving a puff of dust behind. I saw photographers rushing to the gate, cameras aloft. Kokila was getting hysterical. 'I held her closely and recited, rather half-sang in Mandarin, a Chinese quatrain by a medieval Chinese poet. I remember the English translation by Fletcher:

> My lady has rolled up the curtains of pearl
> And sits with a frown on her eyebrows apart
> Wet traces of tears can be seen as they curl
> But who knows for whom is the grief in her heart?

I was caught up in the tragic ambience and my voice came out like a wavering tremolo, high pitched and thin, but rhythmical. I even caught myself swaying a bit. The verse in Chinese seemed to have a soothing effect on Kokila and her hysteria.

The next day she asked me what I had recited.

'It is a Chinese prayer, Kokila, a Chinese prayer in old Mandarin.'

THE LONG NIGHT OF THE BHIKSHU

The evening had moved in on him almost unsuspectingly, grey cloud leading to grey drizzle. It was when the bullfrogs started croaking that he realised it was dark. They were never really vocal while it was light. The pond was a remnant of what was once a jheel, a sort of watering hole for wild elephants. Those days were long past. The jheel had now shrivelled with age, drying slowly at the edges, each sliver of caked mud being grabbed by frantic peasants as they went about adding to their holdings. The village would soon be arriving at the pond, he thought.

He had always known that a day *would* come when his window would open out on nothing. Simply nothing. It bothered him. Nothingness was perhaps something you could put into a void. You couldn't. The void would not be a void if you could place something in it. And one had to distinguish nothingness from somethingness. If nothing was nothing, you really couldn't get hold of it and plonk it someplace—certainly not in a non-existent bowl which went by the name 'void.' He was clutching at the straws of his logic and wouldn't let go.

The Bhikshu started mumbling. It didn't strike him that his speech was a bit slurred and his listener was not attentive. You could not accuse him of lip reading, for the fellow he was speaking to had his back to the Bhikshu. And the Bhikshu was on one of his trips to the past. In his younger days, he was saying, he had wondered about things like whether existence had a hold, however tenuous, on permanence. After all you lived, you ate, drank, loved, died. All this could not be maya or *mithya*. He had left all that behind. All he wanted was tranquillity, the night around him, the chirr of the cicada and the croak of the bullfrog.

For some months now he had grown used to talking to the scarecrow. The guava orchard was an adjunct to his hut and the scarecrow stood there tall and erect and bald, for the raffia had been torn from the coconut shell that passed off for his head. Suppose people overheard? That kind of anxiety flooded his consciousness at times and faded away. It was in the fitness of things that the Bhikshu's scarecrow should be tonsured like a monk.

At first he had been hesitant opening up to the scarecrow. Suppose people heard, they'd think he was mad. Aware that the scarecrow was truly old, older than script perhaps, he wished to speak to him in a dead language. The trouble was he didn't know any dead or dying language, except for a sloka or two and the Gayatri, which in any case he could only mutter to himself, for he was not high enough on the caste ladder to recite it. But that was all in the past tense. He had left those fears behind him as one discards a tattered garment. He had moved on.

He was a latecomer to the Buddha. It was not easy for him to recollect how he came into the fold. It happened. You came upon a stream and drank of its waters. You don't have to explain. You drank because both thirst and water were present at that particular moment. But as he told the scarecrow, even that was not wholly true. Reality is always larger than truth. Yet both fit snugly into each other, truth and reality. He was never sure if the scarecrow had understood.

Every now and then his mind moved into momentary clarity and he would become conscious of the whine and zing of insects, start wondering if he would be there next morning to see the dew glittering on the grass, always presuming there would be dew. A time comes in a man's life when he takes nothing for granted. That moment had arrived for him.

Will and volition had not been his strong suits. His people were not happy. His mother's tongue had clicked like a lizard's. How had doubt leaked into him, she asked. What induced a man to change his gods? There are never any answers to such questions. I haven't changed my gods, Mother, have just moved into a system where there are no gods. How can that be? You can't have a sky without gods—or birds. Don't we all know that Buddha is another avatar of Vishnu? You think your mother is so ignorant, just because she can't sign her name!

He had turned footloose, moving from vihara to vihara, an exile not from his faith so much as from the times, and a family is a part of the times. He moved north towards the mountains. He would work as a farmhand and then get bored with the place and move on. The terraced fields were pale green with rice shoots. The *gompas* took his breath away, the air clean as crystal, gold-painted roofs, gilded pavilions aflutter with pennants, awhirl with prayer wheels. He fell in love with the autumn—amber of the light here. Everyone was friendly, even the Bhotiya dogs. He worked in the buckwheat fields scattered around the *gompa* estate. He got to know the shepherds, even their sheep dogs seemed to recognise him and did not growl. And he picked up lore from the scriptures, and knew all the stories of the past lives of the Sakyamuni. Within some years he became a fixture in the landscape.

A time came when the Abbot changed and the monks started warning him. You will have to give up this, you'll have to give up that. What is life if not full of bonds? But he came to know how the other monks smiled their non-committal smiles, and when cornered, he parted his lips as blandly as they ever did.

He wrote to his mother—it was some years since he had seen her. He wanted to become a bhikshu, he wrote. Alarm bells started ringing in the family. He received letters, never mind if they reached him a month later, asking how he would manage giving up everything. They didn't have a way with words and didn't want to be seen as crude, semi-literate though they were. But he knew what they meant: it was all very well reading the scriptures or closing your eyes and swaying with the prayer wheel. But there was life beyond the pages of a book. He would realise that only when he renounced the world. Renunciation? He had nothing to renounce. If you have nothing, you shed nothing. That's what he wanted to write back, but never did.

Those uneasy dreams of his started two years or so after monkhood. He began hearing voices, mostly his mother calling someone by name, he didn't know who, saw his house crowded with people, string cots laid out in the guava orchard. He dreamt about a woman walking in her dream, her skin grey as chalky clay, her face sand-smudged, her hair dotted with salt crystals. The burnt leaf face of his mother flitted through this dream world, her fragile skin turning to flakes, shredded tissue, moth-wings.

When the dreams stopped abruptly he realised Mother was dead. The Abbot of a sudden one day put his hand on the bhikshu's head and said, 'Son, you've had a trying time,' out of the blue, just like that. That confirmed him in his belief. A year later, calculating from the last time he had dreamt of her, he proceeded to his village, and was not one whit surprised to find he had arrived two days before her *barsi*, death anniversary. He fed the Brahmins, performed all the rites and within a few days left for the *gompa* once again.

This time the solitudes troubled him, the scent of the pine, the wind through the cedars. Things were too clean here, rice fields too lush, the river too blue, river-foam too white. This had nothing to do with reality as he had known down below, poverty and squalor, and it struck him hard. That there was life, this a sojourn in and around the *gompa*, a temporary assignment in paradise. The monks didn't restrain him as he left for his wanderings in the plains.

From one village to another he would walk, the dust of the Doab, fine and powdery, turning to mud on his sweating shins. He would squat under a shady tree and when the villagers would come to him, showing their palms or even horoscopes, he would send them away. He didn't deal in this kind of hocus-pocus, he would tell them. But he would go to their schools and find the school master missing, and start talking to the children and teaching them. People would bring him food. A room would be cleared and made available. He would settle disputes, chant his mantra, move his little prayer wheel and tell stories about the Buddha. The hare story always entranced the children, how the hare, no other than the Buddha in his earlier life, had nothing else to give the anchorite, and so had asked him to prepare a fire, and had offered himself as a meal. And one day, as he moved from hamlet to hamlet, he skirted a jheel which he seemed to remember, entered a village that looked familiar and found he was back home.

The house had gone, for the roof had caved in and one didn't know when the mud wall, scribbled over with moss, would disintegrate. He put up a reed hut and a thatch roof over it. The guava orchard was untouched, and the scarecrow. Talking to the scarecrow, he found, was better than talking to someone in his dream. Mr. Reed-and-Hessian was not a spectre; he occupied space, boasted of an outline, form.

For a brief moment he was aware that he had been babbling away like that mountain brook near the monastery. He was not sure if the scarecrow heard him at all, for the fellow had not turned round even once. There were moments he thought the scarecrow would seek cover from the drizzle and move in and he half expected to hear the swish and rustle of his coming.

The light has to go out when you are fading, but there was no light here in any case. The drizzle had stopped but the trees still dripped. The wind disappeared somewhere in the silence that seemed to engulf the place now. The owl hooted just once. It was no night for his soliloquies. He slept fitfully, his dreams incoherent and suddenly crowded with faces he half remembered. He thought the moon had come out but all that had flickered in his dream was the round face of a tonsured monk. Even that faded, just as dream and sleep and senses were fading. If the rain could walk out of the sky and leave, what was he doing here on terra firma, which was after all just a sense impression? That is what he had been taught at the *gompa*. Images came into his mind and frayed away into nothingness. A crow's nest face stood out, and an arm stretched towards him, the palm shaped like a crow's foot. He wanted to call out 'Mother', half expecting her to come and others to follow, including the scarecrow, still as a Buddha in the stillness of the orchard. Somewhere in the shadowy hinterlands of his fading awareness he half expected to hear the swish and the swirl and the lollop of his coming.

THE DAY OF THE WINTER SOLSTICE

It was Makara Sankranti, the day of the winter solstice by the Hindu calendar, when the sun enters Makara, the sign of Capricorn. Govardhan was sweeping the dry mud floor of his veranda. His sacred thread had been drawn upwards, curling round his left ear. Even though it was a cold January morning, his torso was bare and he had nothing on except his dhoti. After sweeping the floor he squatted facing the east, poured some water in the hollow of his right palm from which he took a sip and invoked all the four Vedas. He started the ritual water-sprinkling, *indriya-sparsha,* over the various parts of his body—mouth, nostrils, eyes, ears, navel, throat, back of the hands. Touching the ground with his third finger, he recited, 'May any evil or trouble which is due to me this day be by thy power prevented.' There was silence for a while as he meditated, his eyes closed in futile concentration. He poured water into his palm again. After a few moments Govardhan launched into the recitations of the Gayatri Mantra, a verse too sacred for women or the lower castes to utter. 'We contemplate the splendid light of the divinity that is the sun; may it illuminate our minds.' And as he ran over the verse again and again, the water slowly drained to the ground from the hollow of his hand.

The battle with his concentration, or rather the lack of it, was a losing one. Not for him the sharp pinpoint focusing of all the faculties of the mind on one object or mantra, to the obliteration of all else. Closing his eyes did not help. Thoughts, anxieties, crowded in like gnats from the river marshes. Concentration at this hour meant struggling against the splendours of daybreak. But today he was taking in everything avidly, the changing colours of the east, the elusive scent of mist, lost even as it was discovered, the shrill percussive chatter of birds, anything that could keep one dread thought away. He had managed to drop the shutters of his mind even as the thought was trying to worm its way in. Sometimes he was not even sure whether it was a dream recall or an image he was conjuring up for himself. A trick of the imagination, perhaps. Words like 'mirage' were not known to a poor Brahmin living on the banks of the Kali Nadi in 1858. But he knew *mithya* and maya and the ambience of these terms, of the falsity and unreality of material form and the illusory nature of existence. He drew solace from both, for he had been battling against this recurring dream about his wife sitting beside a corpse. The flames were soaring up from the funeral pyre, this much the dream vividly recalled. To picture Janaki weeping and taking on all the insignia of widowhood: breaking all her glass bangles, brushing off the sindoor from the parting of her hair, wiping away the red dot on her forehead—these were but extensions of his imagination. Perhaps, he was overwrought because of the dream, which, after one vivid appearance, had come in different guises. Perhaps, he reflected, it was a part of his anxiety about what would happen to her after he died, something every old husband who is really fond of his much younger wife, had to come to terms with.

He had never told Janaki about the dream, even though it had become an obsession with him over the past month. He wanted to communicate with her, but words got in the way.

Come to think of it, he reflected, neither had Janaki ever told him about any dream of hers. No confidences had been shared. She had never let him in.

His pooja over, Govardhan stood up and turned towards the river, gazing at the mists which would soon be dispelled by the rising sun. Not all hues could be codified in words, he thought. Who knew the colour of a range of distant hills, especially if some heat haze from the plains had intervened? The river should be water-blue and the mists white. But here, at the touch of first light, colours shifted like dark panels and the mist looked as green as the water-flow under it. In shadow, the river was as dark as a moleskin.

A flock of honking geese flew past overhead like a length of chainmail clanking away southwards.

In a corner stood a cluster of idols, none higher than six inches, a Vishnu reclining on the back of Sesha Naga, the serpent, a mace-bearing Hanuman and a small image of the goddess—a toy Durga on a toy tiger. He dusted the statuary almost lovingly. He had no children of his own and his attitude to these little images was a mix of adoration and paternal fondness. He folded his hands in front of them and lit an incense stick, contentedly watching its thin tendril of smoke curling upwards, till an almost imperceptible breath of wind wafted it away.

The mists had lifted a little and were levitating now, leaving a clear view of the river. He saw a barge poling away from the eastern bank, his bank, the turban of the boatman visible above the reeds. He saw a string bed being taken down to the river. There was a stir somewhere, with two or three people running towards the bank, one of them holding his sandals in his hands.

Janaki had already started cooking khichdi. He could hear her stirring a ladle in a huge copper bowl streaming over a wood fire. Makara Sankranti was the day the poor came asking for food. You doled out the rice and pulses though God knew that they were just about managing to keep the wolf from the door. It had been a bad year for Govardhan. When the grain had to be sown there was no one to plough the land. Boys, who would have worked on the land for a month for a head-load of paddy, had other things to do these past six months. Some had gone off to Fatehgarh, where they watched the various processions in the city or stood gawking at the Englishmen who were shot in the parade square. Others were excitedly watching the alarums and excursions, the arrival and departure of mutinous troops from Mainpuri and Bewar, Sitapur and Shahjahanpur. He had wanted to put his own shoulder to the plough, but Janaki had resisted fiercely. This had never happened, not in seven generations, on either her side or his. A Brahmin is never known to have ploughed a field. All the rest of his agrarian labours a poor Brahmin would gladly undertake, hoeing, digging, pulling out weeds or cutting a water channel and irrigating the fields. There was no bar to harvesting either, and you could flail away with the scythe till your arm fell off your shoulder and your feet and ankles bled as you walked over the stubble. But ploughing, no. That was done by other people who, according to the accepted mythology of caste origins, had sprung from Purusha's biceps, or thighs, or feet, but had not sprouted from his head, as the Brahmin had.

He had listened to her rasping protestations for a fortnight, by which time sowing had been greatly delayed. Then he went off to the fields much before first light, and started ploughing. Two hours a day, or rather night, by moonlight and lantern light he worked the plough for the best part of a week. Normally it should not have taken Janaki a moment to see through the obvious stratagem. His palm itself should have given him away, blistered as it was with holding the *muthiya*, the handle of the plough, too hard. But Janaki had been busy. All that toing and froing of the mutineers had fascinated her, as they had thundered in and out of the village in a cloud of dust and a trail of excited children. She would dart down to the village whenever she had the chance and listen keenly to the gossip, of troop movements, of proclamations of the Moghul emperor or the Nawab of Farrukhabad. She would meet up with people who had actually heard the town-crier shouting in the streets. '*Khalq Khuda ki, mulk Badshah ka, hukum Nawab Rais Bahadur ka*, the earth is the Lord's, the country that of the Emperor and authority the Nawab's.' She would even at times go down to the village in the afternoons, leaving her guava grove to the birds, when they were most prone to attack the fruit.

Govardhan had kept aloof from all this. The distance between the village and his house, perched atop a sand cliff overlooking the river, helped him stay away. He was unhappy that after fifteen years of marriage she should still behave like a child, a village urchin almost. This was not a tamasha, a troupe of tribal acrobats who had come to the village to display their antics, or some conjuror with dancing bears or cavorting baboons. The mutiny was serious business. Govardhan wanted to keep his thoughts away from it, the rights and wrongs of it, and while he was all for the British to be thrown out, he had reservations on troopers killing their own officers. The shoals of his morality were unclear and murky. His morality was confined to a little world of touch and taboo. As long as no mlechcha or Muslim or *firangi* came in contact with him, so long as he could bathe in the river and intone his dawn prayers, he was happy. But he was soon to realise that one was part of the collective karma, and if blood and mayhem were all around, you could not remain unaffected.

☛

One morning in early October a cavalry trooper shambled into his house, two bearded flunkies in tow. He had a scarlet coat and trousers of black broadcloth. The man was tall and burly and had a frighteningly long moustache. He had walked in through the open door, crossed a mud-floored room into the verandah where the idols lay in a corner, and plonked himself on a string bed which had been laid out in the shade of a peepal tree. The two sepoys stood beside him on either side. Govardhan had followed, utterly alarmed by the way the man had walked in.

'Maharaj! Maharaj!' he had cried, his tone combining dismay, amazement and protest in equal measures. 'This is the house of a Brahmin!'

One of the flunkies held his arm and asked, 'Do you know who he is?'

'Let him be anybody! This is the house of a Brahmin! You do not enter it at will. You do not enter wearing leather boots!'

'This is Risaldar Ram Khilawan.'

The name meant nothing to Govardhan, but he realised the flunkies held him in awe. There was no chair in his house, and he was determined not to squat on the floor in front of this Risaldar. So he stood there, proudly staring at the intruder with all the haughtiness that he could command. A minute later he was surprised to see Janaki coming out and asking the man if he wanted some water! He would never have believed it. Ram Khilawan demurred. She brought him a glass nonetheless. He drank the water gratefully in large, noisy gulps. She observed his adam's apple working away as the water went down his gullet. When he finished she did not go back but stood there, glass in hand, her head covered by the pallu of her saree. He noticed the flicker of excitement in her eyes as she observed the cavalry boots reaching up to his knees and his scarlet tunic.

'What is your name, pandit?'

'Govardhan.'

'You are a lucky man, Govardhan.'

What did the man mean? Surely, he didn't have the temerity to refer to Janaki's good looks in front of him? God knew she was beautiful, but could anyone be brazen enough to say it to her, or worse, his face.

'There is no higher feature this side of the river than your house. You could be the first to notice the *firangi* army when it nears the Kali Nadi.'

The *firangi*? The army? Nothing could have sounded more weird to Govardhan.

'We are no idlers, Maharaj. I work in the fields and often have to go across the river. My wife keeps the birds away from the guava trees there. And you can very well see how far we are from the village. It is almost half a *kos*. Whom will I run to? This is beyond me. You don't need a poor Brahmin like me to tell you about an approaching army. The buzzards will tell you that as they wheel and wait upon the leftovers from its kitchens. Don't worry. An army doesn't move by stealth. It proclaims itself to the earth and the skies.'

Ram Khilawan had gone, as he had come in, without a greeting or a salutation. But he came again. And again. He avoided the track that ran through the village. He would leave his horse with his flunkies at the river bank and climb the sand cliff. This way he avoided causing excitement among the village urchins and the village curs. He came in the afternoons mostly, when Govardhan would have gone across the river to his cronies in Isanpur, and Janaki was in the guava grove. She would be sitting on a string bed, pulling a rope tied to a can hoisted over a tree fork. Each tug at the rope created din enough to scare the birds out of the sky, leave alone the orchard.

'Why don't you put up a scarecrow here?' he asked her once.

'Why put a scarecrow when you are around in person?' It took her a few minutes to control her laughter, so overcome was she with her own joke. He joined in the laughter, drawing her close to him.

☛

By noon a goatherd and a boatman from the ferry had gorged themselves on Janaki's khichdi. A mendicant carried his share away in his bowl. It was time to move out, thought Govardhan, as he wrapped himself in a frayed white shawl and strode down to the river. It was a problem that most of his friends lived across it.

'Why couldn't you have friends this side of the river?' Janaki had asked a few days after they were married.

'Because I do *not* have friends this side of the river,' he answered with some asperity.

His friends were other Brahmins living in Isanpur Kalan (big) and Isanpur Khurd (small), two adjacent villages lying on a huddle across the Kali Nadi. There, amidst horoscopes and palm imprints, hours would go by in gossip. Cattle markets, crops, bandits, elopements and mistresses would all be discussed. Govardhan had not been across the river since the battle had been fought, a week or so earlier. He started on his trip, holding a stick in his right hand

and the folds of his dhoti in his left, descending briskly. A villager and a beggar woman met him on the way, both stopping in their tracks and saluting him respectfully. Of late he could see in other people's faces that he was getting old. As people accosted him on the road, palms seemed to fold earlier in salutation. From the women, especially the young, he received that quick deferential bow and the sudden lowering of eyes, as if something tangible had been dropped on the ground right under his feet.

At the ferry he walked gingerly like a cat not wanting to wet its feet. The boatman who always took him free across the river (he wouldn't dream of ever charging a Brahmin) extended his hand and half lifted and half pulled him in. What rough hands! He remembered the hands of his mother, which fairly crackled when she caressed his face. All those years of scrubbing vessels, stoking wood fires and pulling the rope pail up the well shaft had taken their toll. The first time he took Janaki's hands in his he had been thrilled. How soft, how silken, how different from the dry-leaf hands of his mother.

The far bank of the river was covered with reeds. He came to a clearing where he found two boys scurrying back and forth, bringing in firewood and piling it up. A tall peepal, hollowed out by ants, marked the spot. Another furtive funeral, he thought, some sepoy or subedar who would soon be going up in flames. Govardhan quickened his step because he did not want to get caught up in this. His memory was poor and he could not rattle off the slokas as a pandit should. He walked another twenty minutes or so along a thin foot track that went through the reedy undergrowth, till he emerged into the fields. The yellow refrain of mustard flower was everywhere, and the sharp tang that went with it. Reaching his friend Tripathi's house, he skipped the usual long-drawn pleasantries. He wanted to be done with business before his host's other cronies turned up, as they normally did, during late afternoon.

'I have something important which can't wait. Please fish out my horoscope first and try and give me a short, straight answer! Do you see any indication of imminent death? If so, how much time do I have?'

Tripathi gave him a long, quizzical look. 'This is a difficult question, especially these days. Sometimes one can lose faith in astrology, you know. Do you think that all those who died in battle barely ten days back had it coming to them in their horoscopes? A thousand lives terminate at the same moment. Was all this written in their stars, cannon and Kali Nadi, death by sabre-thrust or bullet or just a fall from a fleeing horse? Do you think, Govardhan, that the gods had the time to script all this minutiae into a thousand destinies? However, yours is another matter. I will try to answer you.'

Tripathi gazed long at the horoscope, calculated the position of Saturn on it, and of the two ascending and descending nodes, the baleful Rahu and the comet-like Ketu. He shook his head. 'No, you have quite a few years yet. What made you panic?'

'I've been getting this dream almost every other week, Tripathi. Each time I see Janaki a widow there.'

Tripathi got out her horoscope as well and, after a proper scrutiny, dismissed the idea. She had brought him luck, another five years to his life, at least.

Tripathi's friends trooped in but the atmosphere did not liven up. Rumours of villagers being strung up on the roads by the British column which had set out from Allahabad to relieve Kanpur had reached the district. Who could ensure against a repeat performance here? There was tension in the air and speculation was rife. What would happen to the Nawab of Farrukhabad, who had raised the banner of revolt and announced the takeover of the area by drumbeat? What about the Kotwal, the senior upholder of law in the district who had a hand in many of the killings of the Sahibs? And what was in store for the rebel troops? This being Govardhan's first visit in a fortnight, he could hardly wait to fire off a volley of questions.

'What really happened? Were they outnumbered?'

'Were *who* outnumbered?'

'The Telungas—sepoys—of course.'

'Why don't you say *us*?' asked one of Tripathi's friends. 'You talk as if you belong to a different people.'

Govardhan was not going to take a beating in this battle of pronouns. 'Because,' he said angrily, 'I am *not* a Telunga! I wouldn't have done any of the things *they* did, slaughtering women and all the rest. First you take employment with the mlechcha, then you wear leather boots, you cross the seas, eat with a man squatting barely a yard from you without the faintest idea about his *biradari*! And when you have lost your caste and all the merit that your forefathers gained for you, you strike out against your masters! Had they killed before losing their caste one could have said they did it for dharma. But all this bloodshed now was merely a spillover of baser passions. And to what purpose? They will in any case be reborn as dogs or hyenas.'

A silence descended on the room for some time. Tripathi took up Govardhan's initial question.

'You want to know what happened?' he asked. 'Well, the battle was lost because of an untrained horse.'

The others kept smoking their chillums impassively. Not a flicker of expression on any of the weather-beaten faces.

'You don't expect me to believe that?'

'Ask anyone. You see the *firangi* cavalry kept attacking the square which the sepoys had formed. The horses were trained to charge at a square and then dash aside. You can't have the cavalry mowing down the infantry on the parade ground, can you? Well, the horses behaved exactly that way in actual battle, and veered away till this sergeant, on a huge untrained horse, pierced the square like Abhimanyu piercing the ranks of the Kauravas. The others followed, and the battle was over!'

An hour before dusk Govardhan got up. It wouldn't do to delay his departure any longer. One responded to unsettled times with settled ways. He wanted to be home before dark. As he left Isanpur, silence descended on him like a palpable presence. People had gone into hiding all over the countryside. The wounded were especially spirited away in forgotten hamlets, where some were recuperating and others were taking their time on the long road of dying.

As he left the mustard fields behind, and reed and bulrush took over, three men fell in step with him. He had seen them around earlier, two boatmen from a nearby village, and another who was taller and sturdier than the two, someone he had seen before but could not place.

'Panditji, come with us.'

He found the voice remotely familiar. Where had he heard it? At a market or at the ferry? His mind was in a whirl now. He did not like the suddenness of the encounter—these men had been waiting for him. Without as much as a touch he found himself being propelled towards another direction. Of course, he was being led towards the clearing. A sudden gust of wind carried a woman's grief to him, a tattered bit of sound torn from a prolonged wail; a woman crying for a lost son, a husband, a father perhaps. Was there something about the timbre of the voice that was familiar? All wails are similar, floating on a raft of high-pitched octaves. The wind dropped, and with it the lament. What did they need? What could a poor pandit do for them, he asked.

'We need you at a funeral, Panditji. Someone has to read the prayers, you know, how else would the soul be liberated?'

He could hear the croak of the reed frogs now. The river may have flowed here once, but it had regressed long back, leaving a mosaic of ponds behind. A crane startled him as it came in to land, its long stilt-legs held out in front to take in the shock, its wings gently folding in like a concertina. It was coming in from the river to roost somewhere here. The tall man tried to shoo the crane away, but the bird couldn't be bothered. Govardhan was trying hard to think who the man was and where he had seen him. Memory would not focus on him, just as it was unable to focus on the voice which the wind had carried to him. A sudden twist in the track brought the hollowed out peepal in view. There on a bed of twigs, stalks of dry reeds and firewood lay the huge corpse of Ram Khilawan. His face had been made hideous by a large scar that ran across the head right up to the eyebrow, a solid sword-blow, if ever there was one. He looked as large in death as he did in life. Cyanosis had added an impasto or two to his swarthy skin. The thickets of his moustache were as frightening as ever. The dead Kumbha Karna would have looked something like him. The very sight of the man made Govardhan delve into demonology.

Besides him sat a woman weeping, now and then banging her head against the firewood. Her right arm lay listless over Ram Khilawan's knees and her hair, unbraided like a virago's, fell from side to side as she rocked in lament. Her grief was intense and there seemed something eerily and terribly familiar about the figure. He suddenly recalled that the tall man with him was one of

Ram Khilawan's flunkies who had accompanied him on his first visit to the house. A boy, naked till the waist, started pouring ghee over the wood, so that the corpse sizzled the better once the pyre was lit. The woman lifted her head from the bier. Even though her hair was spread maenad-like behind her, there was no mistaking her. Of course, this was Janaki. If it was his dream which was to be made flesh, as it were, if it had to be enacted in real life, like an arrow which had left the bowstring and had to fall on someone, he wished it had fallen on him. Both Janaki and he would have been spared the shame, had he, Govardhan, died. How happy this cavalry trooper or Risaldar, or whatever he was, must have made her (this man with a moustache running wild over half an acre), for Janaki to be plunged into this kind of grief now. Whatever the astrologer may have said, Janaki sat there, effectively widowed. He could not cope with the enormity of it all. The look in his eyes froze like water stunned into ice.

WHEN GANDHI CAME TO GORAKHPUR

As Shadilal was about to stride out of his house, he remembered to put his wallet carefully in his coat pocket. It was a closed-collar coat, worn on top of his dhoti. He wrapped a muffler round his head, not so much against the January cold as against too easy recognition. Through force of habit he peeped into his backyard where both his cows were tethered under a canopy of corrugated tin. Some termite-eaten logs were piled in a corner, ready for the cooking fires. A whiff of bran, fodder and dung came to his nostrils as he retreated from his makeshift cattle shed back into the veranda. The *mehri* who cleaned the vessels was already banging on the rear door, clamouring for entrance, though it was still dark. He stepped out, walking briskly, turning left at the first crossing into a blind vista of neem trees fading into the morning fog. The road led to a Shiva temple, but that was not where he was going. He turned abruptly left once again, and looked the other way as he passed his favourite paan shop, where the *tambolia* was splashing water on his kiosk. Must be mad, Shadilal thought, messing around with water in this cold. Who would buy betel at this hour, anyway?

The early morning sights registered themselves on his brain with remarkable clarity; a temple priest hurrying from the well, dripping wet, perhaps already late for the morning lustrations of the idol; a bullock cart trundling unerringly towards the grain market, though the cart owner, wrapped in his blanket, had fallen asleep; the snarling dialectic of two growling dogs confronting each other near a garbage bin.

He could not shake off the thought of the termite-eaten logs in his backyard. When the logs first arrived at half the price of normal firewood, he had noticed how desperately the ants scrambled away the moment some logs were placed in the fire. He too was now sneaking away, like wood lice from rotting timber.

Shadilal left the streets behind him, homing straight for the railway station. He had a clear view of the eastern sky now, one brief purple streak overhanging a charcoal dawn. Purple. The word brought unhappy memories. Only the other day he had been ticked off in court by the magistrate. 'Cut the purple prose out, will you, Mr Shadilal,' he had snapped, 'and get down to brass tacks.' Later, as if that was not enough, he had said, 'Stop going round in circles and come to the point. What exactly are you getting at?' If only he knew. There were occasions when he just talked on, hoping some sudden inspiration would clear the cobwebs in his brain.

The railway station, wrapped in a shawl of mist, seemed somnolent. No engine-hoot, no whistle from the guard.

'Is the train on time?' he asked at the ticket booth.

'On time? It is there on the platform, *Babuji*! Can't you hear the hustle-bustle?'

He pronounced the last two words as *hustalbustal*.

Suddenly, as if someone had pulled out his ear plugs, all the sounds came through, passengers summoning porters, hawkers shouting, the scrape of sandals, the flap, flap, flap of chappals striking against the heels of feet and sounding distinctly like wing beats. The Avadh-Tirhut Mail stood there, the engine throwing jets of steam in the air. He bought a newspaper and ensconced himself in the corner of an Inter-Class Compartment. He spread out the paper in front of him, his eye flitting from headline to headline, unable to rest anywhere. The paper screened his face from prying eyes. Vakil Sahib was, after all, well known. A chance meeting with a client or an acquaintance would have been disastrous. The eight leaves of the *National Herald* spread out in front acted like a face mask.

The platform vendors were doing brisk business, ladling out chickpeas in leaf plates stitched into inverted cones, or serving tea in unglazed earthenware *kullars*. His co-passengers were slurping their tea. He heard the crash of *kullars* as they were hurled on the track. Someone clanged on a hanging rail, reminding him of school, reminding him of jail. Only here the clanging was urgent, insistent, not measured strokes to toll the hour. He could not keep his head buried in the paper once the train steamed out. Telegraph poles started slipping by. A sal forest went past as if on wheels. The wizened old hunchback at the railway crossing, the blue-turbaned signal man looking down from the cabin; slabs of forest turned into sliding panels; engine-smoke billowing back, honed blue by the morning mist; a wheat field fenced in by cacti; a dead tree in the middle of another wheat field. Why had they let that tree remain there? A people hugging their dead trees and dead gods. It was the same with legal codes, he thought. Regrettably, Manu rather than Macaulay held sway.

He disembarked at the first stop, Khalilabad. As he came down the platform, happy in his anonymity, a voice called out, 'What brings you here, Vakil Sahib?' Legs braced, hands folded in front, woollen shawl draped over his shoulder—where had he seen the fellow before? Yes of course, 'State *vs* Thakur Ramprasad.' The deceased and Ram had swung their lathis at each other over some cattle-trespass in field, and *crack*—Ram's stick had landed on the other's skull. The police had tried to run him down for murder. If they had confined the charge to grievous hurt or even attempt-to-murder, he would have gone to jail. Shadilal's own contribution at the trial had not exactly been electrifying. The Public Prosecutor had talked of Ram Khilawan's enmity with the deceased.

'Objection, Your Honour!' he had shouted, 'Ramprasad hit Kade Din.'

'I have no quarrel with that', said the Prosecutor rather patiently. But when he again made a reference to the attack on the deceased, Shadilal's protest had been shriller.

'Your Honour, when Kade Din was hit on the head, he was not the deceased! He became "deceased" only after he died!'

Premeditated murder was too ridiculous a charge.

'You mean to say, P.P. Sahib,' the bald-headed Judge asked the Public Prosecutor, 'that the accused had conspired with the cattle of the deceased to trespass into his field so that an altercation would ensue and he could conveniently kill Kade Din?' He threw the case out.

Now the same Thakur Ramprasad stood there, eyeing Shadilal keenly.

'I thought today was your big day in Gorakhpur, Vakil Sahib.'

'What big day? Whose day? Mind your business.' Ramprasad bowed to Shadilal, and the lawyer strode out in a huff.

After shaking off his erstwhile client, he wandered aimlessly in the town. He drank a glass of buttermilk at a *halwai's*, sitting on a bench along with other riff-raff. It was getting warm now and he couldn't keep the muffler wrapped around his head. More chances of getting recognised, he thought. He saw a thin, almost tubercular Muslim with a skull cap and a wispy beard. A few seconds later he heard the noon azan and felt unreal. Surely that short little maulvi couldn't have climbed up the minaret in those ten seconds or so? The faithful did not seem to respond. It was a call which had got lost somewhere on a forgotten minaret.

No one was answering calls these days. He himself had evaded Gandhi's call at the last moment.

The word Gandhi had come like a double beat upon this kettledrum country. To a nation scavenging for a philosophy, something indigenous, with a touch of the top knot as it were, and not merely borrowed from nineteenth-century British liberals, Gandhi was the obvious answer. It wasn't Western civilisation, soft-wheeled on a trolley that he was bringing to you. It was regular Indian homespun. And yet revolutionary enough, thought Shadilal. The fellow could defy Manu! Some guts! Like himself, a lawyer, nothing more. Yes, Gandhi had gone to England, Lincoln's Inn and all that, and Shadilal had not. Ten years his senior in age, that's all. And here, in January 1921, Gandhi was coming to Gorakhpur, while he, Shadilal, had broken his word to him.

Well, not exactly. He had not made his pledge to Gandhi personally, had he? You could twist it any way you please.

Gandhi's stature was not longer than history as yet. Nor had a staunch band of followers gathered round him like the Galilean disciples around Christ. But he was already dreaming for the whole country, and what he dreamt today became reality the day after. Yes, Shadilal admired the man. He would save us from blood spillage and the conspiratorial murmur of knives rubbing against whetstones.

He checked his thoughts. They were inevitably leading to guilt. Once you let guilts cut their milk teeth, you never know what they would start chewing on next. The more you praise Gandhi, the worse will it get for you, he told himself. Shadilal had missed lunch. He walked into a municipal park and ensconced himself on a stone bench in the sun. He had to kill time, desperately almost. Somehow get through till dark and then take that passenger train back, the one which halted at almost every unlit flag station. Yes, by then the bonfire would be over. Satin and twill, worsted and flannel and tweed would all be turned to cinders in one of those bonfires of foreign textiles that were smouldering all over India. Only Shadilal's black bands and his lawyer's coat would not be in it. That was supposed to be the piece de resistance of the whole show, the advocate abandoning his (alas, not very lucrative) practice, and doffing his black coat to applause and slogans. Everything was being turned into a public spectacle after all; politics, like religion, being reduced to a series of vast symbolic gestures. And now he had reneged. Broken his pledge. As he sat there in inert repose, the wound ached. This much-dreamt-of day was slowly silting away like sand in an hourglass.

He walked over to drink water at a handpump. Around it was slush. He worked the hand crank and drank, one hand cupped under his lips. He slipped for an instant and one foot went ankle-deep into the mud. Water bubbled up, like an old sorrow suddenly surfacing. As the day had drawn near Shadilal's panic had increased. How would he manage once he gave up his practice? Would he have to move back to his village? Then the Magistrate, Douglas Wright, had asked him over to his chambers.

'What's this I hear, Mr Shadilal? One hears of strange goings-on, of confabulations with Congressmen and what have you. I believe you are going to burn your bar licence and your law degree? I wouldn't like to be seen burning my boats or my bridges, if you understand what I mean. This is a time for testing our friends. We always take good care of them. Well, if it comes to that, we could take care of our enemies as well.'

The message had gone home. For a week after that he had been in a terrible dither. Wearing an exaggerated frown on his face he went to see his colleague, Pashupati Nath. They got to discussing Shadilal's future. Shadilal started expressing his concern about the cases he was handling. What would happen to his clients? Whom would they go to? Would Pashupati Nath favour him by taking his old cases? Nath understood the pitch instinctively.

'I would not mind taking up your cases, but my hands are full. The lawyer's dharma enjoins that your first duty is towards your clients,' he said rather ponderously. '*Moakil* first, Gandhi afterwards.' Pashupati went on in this vein. 'A fine kettle of fish we have here. An advocate throws his underwear into a bonfire. All right, all right, his coat into the fire. An innocent man hangs by the neck till he is dead. There is no rational nexus between these two events. But you know and I know that there is a nexus. A man hangs because he has not been properly defended!' Pashupati's statement gave Shadilal what he needed, a righteous veneer for his plan of action.

The 8:00 pm 'Passenger' took Shadilal back to Gorakhpur, the engine hooting and coughing all the way. At home he pretended as if nothing had happened, tidying up his court papers and filling ink into his fountain pen. His wife looked at him enquiringly once, but never opened her mouth, waiting for him to speak first.

'I hope my coat is ironed.'

She noticed that he was looking down at his papers though he did not have his glasses on. 'Which coat?'

'The black coat! The one I wear to court every day!'

'I gave that away. The Congressmen came asking for it in the evening. The degrees as well. Though when I took them out of the trunk, I found that white ants had been among them.'

Shadilal did not want his agitation to be visible to his wife and made a great effort to control himself. To chide her now would mean losing her respect for good. How do you tell your wife that you have chickened out at the last moment, withdrawn from the brink, just when you were about to make that heroic leap; that you will now play the game according to the rules laid down by your foreign masters; become once again a part of their infernally creaking system of justice, where everyone swears to tell the truth and each person lies; become another squeak in that eternal debating society which the British were pleased to call their courts of law?

Next morning he had his usual cold-water bath; but he put on a well-starched dhoti and, wrapping himself in a dun-coloured shawl, set out to meet the Mahatma. It was still dark and lights were on in the house where Gandhi was staying. Shadilal folded his hands, bowed and sat down cross-legged on a white sheet which had been spread out on the stone floor. Gandhi was concentrating on trundling his spinning wheel. From a distance of five feet, the tradesman showed through his features, a mercantile ancestry rather than the apostlehood being thrust on him by the masses. After five long minutes Gandhi looked up smiling, his eyes sparkling through those round-rimmed spectacles of his.

'So you are the shy lawyer?' he said.

Shadilal mumbled his assent, in an unintelligible manner.

'What makes you so shy?' asked Gandhi.

'Shy, shy, shy,' poor Shadilal repeated in agreement, at a loss for words, writhing in embarrassment.

Gandhi worked his wheel for another five minutes, giving the other man an opportunity to regain his composure.

'You know, I understand you perfectly well,' he said, looking him in the eye, compassion written all over his slightly wrinkled face. 'There was a time when I used to be as tongue-tied as you are right now. Words would come to mind but they refused to roll off the tongue.'

There was a titter from the half dozen women sitting on the floor, and the tension eased for Shadilal. He was intuitively getting the drift of the conversation.

'Actually,' said Gandhi, 'we have both joined the wrong profession, you know. No gift of the gab, as the English would put it. As if law was not bad enough, I have moved into politics. But it is not myself I wanted to talk about. You haven't answered my question.'

'What question?' he asked timidly.

'You have a knack for avoiding awkward questions. You wouldn't fare too well in the witness box, though as a lawyer you might be getting by. I simply asked you what made you so shy.'

Half a dozen answers thronged to his brain simultaneously, but none could get past his tongue. A local politician, sitting there with the others, bailed him out, little realising that this impulsive gesture of his would give birth to a rival politician who would edge him out of the cabinet one day.

'Perhaps you don't know, Bapu, Shadilal's parents died when he was still in school.'

It was time for his morning walk. Gandhi stood up. A covey of young women scurried to the door, but Gandhi ignored them.

'How strong are your shoulders?' he asked Shadilal, as they walked out.

'They will become strong, sir, were you to lean on them.'

'I will,' said the great man, putting his hand on Shadilal's shoulder and walking towards the still faltering light of the east.

BARS

We dropped the subject we were discussing when the subject walked in. Five minutes earlier she had said, 'The expression on this Jailor's face is always satirical.'

'How many Jailors have you seen?'

'Just this one.'

'And how often have you seen him?'

'Twice.'

'And that makes you so certain, geometry class… end of theorem. He's just like any other Jailor—that's his job, keeping people within bars.'

'Behind, you mean.'

'I prefer within. Incidentally I have never heard of satire being parked on a face, even if it belongs to an unfortunate Jailor. Anger, yes, cruelty too; such attributes get etched on a face perhaps, eye and the turn of the lip giving a man away. But satire?'

I could see the anger in her eyes. 'Correction, it is not jailors who are unfortunate, it is the ones they jail!' Feisty girl. Pointless telling her, I thought, that jailors don't jail, it's the courts. She would know that but what do you do about passion, anger.

'Let's face it, you had made up your mind before you saw him, isn't it? You thought of a jailor as someone louche, sinister, possibly with an eye patch, no?'

'No!' she barked.

And here he was, the Jailor I mean. 'O here you are again,' he said looking at his wrist as the watch came out sliding through his cuffs. He pretended not to notice me, just looked at Gabriela and nodded. 'Still a half hour, you know. I could let you see him, but visiting hours are sacrosanct, as you know.'

'I don't.' Stubborn angry look, eyes squarely meeting the Jailor's. These young girls, so ready to pick up fights! Gabriela was not one to be cowed down; what if her uncle was in the tub and Authority Incarnate stood there, a baton tucked under his armpit.

'Well, rules are sacred and so are Visiting Hours.'

'Why should rules stand between niece and uncle or daughter and father?'

'Because rules are rules, Lady, stern and immovable, like bricks, fired in a kiln.' He nodded rather kindly at her and walked off; didn't want to be interrogated by this aggressive girl. Interrogation was not a nice word in Jail, reeked of illegality, cops barging in at odd hours and 'interrogating' prisoners.

The Jailor's look is nondescript, the colour of his face colourless. A job requirement I thought when I first called on him on my transfer as the new Jail doctor. His office was a few yards away from the main building. An old Jail it is, weather-beaten and mouldy, with thick walls and sharp battlements, a once-imposing edifice in a princely state in what was then known as Central Provinces. His office looked modern though, with chessboard tiles and steel tables.

'Look after them,' he told me pointing to the inmates inside, 'they need you. We can't do much for them but at least we can look after their physical health.' For the next few months those were the only sympathetic words I heard from him. Whether he had a soft chord somewhere, I had no idea. 'One thing more, I would like you to wander around the meeting place during visiting hours. Don't misunderstand, not to ferret out what transpires between inmates and visitors, but to keep a finger on the pulse generally. You don't have to tell me, I am not asking you to snoop. As for hardened criminals, murderers and kidnappers, I have my ways of knowing what is going on.'

I was about to get up, but he kept silent, grimly lost in thought. Then he added, 'The Deputy Jailor is no good. I will have to lean on you at times.'

Two people landed an hour earlier always, Gabriela, the niece of Father Baptista and Aadila, wife of the 'terrorist' Abrar Hasan. The terrorist bit had started being downplayed when another investigating agency had taken over the case. The press was saying that the whole group was innocent and the new investigators thought so. He had been four years with us. We in the jail know that between what the police and the courts say and the jailbird's version there's not just a gulf but an ocean. Aadila hardly said anything interesting. She just repeated each time that Abrar was a head mechanic at a big service station and one day the cops came and took him away. He was innocent.

Gabriela, who after a meeting or two had asked me to call her Gaby, as everyone else did, was just too angry to talk about her uncle's case. I also never probed. One never knew about her temper. The Deputy Jailor had got a mouthful from her once. When I asked her she said, 'The fool tells me, why do you come to see your uncle? Why not his wife or daughter? Because, I told the fool, my uncle is a Catholic priest. He can't have a wife and so he can't have a daughter! Have you understood that? He stared at me vilely but didn't say anything!'

I decided to ask Father Baptista one day. He was given a cell and a decent cot, allowed food from home every now and then. The Jailor even allowed him his own clothes in the cell, but when he came out for his constitutional he had to be in 'stripes', our prescribed jail attire. And he had the use of a mobile phone—all this went unappreciated by Gaby. Ungrateful people! He was even allowed paper to write on, though there's a story to it. For when the new Deputy Minister came to have a look at the Jail (he called it 'inspection'—though we never got an inspection report) he went into the 'paper business' as he described it.

'No diary, *shiary*, you understand! I don't want inmates writing gory story—bad food, *maar peet* in jail, drug, charas. MLAs ask questions. They have nothing else to do. Only allow to write slokas.'

The jailor intervened. 'Sir, what about Christians and others? Can they quote from their books?'

'Not understanding! Only slokas!'

Talking with Father Baptista was rewarding. He was tall, shaggy-haired, spoke excellent Hindustani, had no trouble sitting cross-legged, Indian style on his cot; didn't look the proselytising type. I asked for a chair, which was brought in.

He was a good talker. 'Do you get bored?' I asked him.

'Now and then. I try to keep myself busy in prayer to our Lord, but even prayer has to end sometime. And then how much can the mind wander and forage for memory, sponge on it? But these ten months have not been very hard, if that's what you want to know.'

I tried to convince him that this was simple conversation, I wasn't keen to know anything. Have no idea how much he believed me. His looks betrayed nothing. I presume it is a quality which only those few possess, who serve God. I was unhappy to see some of the lower staff keep an eye on uncle and niece as they talked through the grill during meeting hours. What were they looking for, sign talk, inflection of brow, a blank look, a Morse code of expressions? Or perhaps they were watching for the transmission of a dark thought from one to another.

Slowly over weeks I zeroed in. What brought him here, in the tub? Surely you know all that, he said. The whole town knows. There was nothing to it. This man by name Sunil Manohar came to the church and said his father had died. He wanted him to be buried in our Christian cemetery. The man looked under the weather with two day's stubble. He looked distressed. I asked him if he was a Christian? No he said. What about your father? He smiled. 'If I am not a Christian obviously my father will not be a Christian?' Not necessary I thought but I nodded. No point arguing. 'Why do you want him buried? Why can't you take him to the burning ghat?'

Straight question. He, meaning his father, wanted his body to be interred here. The man was always in mortal dread of fire—he carried a few burns from his childhood. You can't really argue with that. And our cemetery looked good, a small island of stone crosses, with bougainvillea draped on the enclosing wall. I had been entrusted with two novitiates who were on their way to becoming priests. The Bishop wanted me to assess their beliefs and desire to take the plunge. As you know it involves celibacy, tough decision for modern men. These youngsters had enough sense to advise me against the burial, but they couldn't give a convincing rationale. I saw no harm. In most things we have very little say. Fate decides them for us. But surely a man could decide what happens to his outer shell after he is dead.

Next morning I conducted the skimpiest of ceremonies. You can't let a man go into the earth without a prayer surely! I read a short prayer from the 3:1-9 *Book of Wisdom*,

> He accepted them as a holocaust.
> The souls of the virtuous are in the hands of God,
> No torment shall ever touch them.
> In the eyes of the unwise, they did appear to die,
> Their going looked like a disaster,
> their leaving us like an annihilation;
> But they are in peace ....

I was especially keen on one line in this prayer which read 'their hope was rich with immortality.'

'Was that all you read?' I asked.

'One other passage. I couldn't refrain from reading out from the *Acts of the Apostles:*

> Peter addressed Cornelius and his household: "The truth I have now come to realise" he said, "is that God does not have favourites, but that anybody of any nationality who fears God and does what is right is acceptable to him."

That was all. It was a short service if that's what you can call it. I hope you know, Doctor, that in a church service we consider Jesus sacramentally present. By the evening someone complained. The constabulary came with a sub-Inspector in tow, or vice versa, talked of this and that and after two hours of futile questions arrested me. It was the anti-conversion law of the state. I told them we were not converting anyone. Someone wanted to be buried in our cemetery; we buried him. That was all. But would they listen. It's ten months now since ...' he shrugged his shoulders.

I felt like assuaging him and asked, 'Hope things are okay here?'

He nodded. 'Yes, thank you, but they wouldn't allow other inmates here to come to me. They thought I'd convert them!'

It was rumination time on occasions. He would close his eyes and start reminiscing. Once he said I am not sure if I am a good believer. I am not sure at all if St. Thomas the Apostle ever came to India but I dare not say that to a Catholic from Kerala. I have been to a seminary for a course with members of the Syro-Malabar Church. There were also St. Thomas Christians there, they call themselves Nasranis, a Syrian term meaning followers of the Nazarene. I couldn't last in a church in South India for more than a month, I am sure. Belief has to be absolute, blind—no place for the rational in it. That's the terrible danger in reasoning. How could a first century rickety boat set out say from Jaffa or Tyre or wherever and make it to Malabar? And hardly a reference in any chronicle! Doubt is the Devil. You believe in the divine just as you believe the earth is round. Lack of belief gets mapped on the face, however much you may dissemble. It is something people of my calling need to be wary of.

Sometime back I had asked him what he would do once he got back; was there anything particular he yearned for? Let's face it, inane questions. One could ask that of anyone in Jail. 'All I want is quiet around me,' he said, 'silence thick as fog, silence that you could cut with a knife. Too much hustle-bustle here in this place. (He never called our jail by its name.) Too much of coming and going, unlocking of cells, food passed through little openings, guards talking loudly when they are not shouting at the prisoners, aimless rounds by your officials. I just want some greenery around me and quiet, the silence even more important than the greenery.'

Father Baptista was worried about one inmate—Abrar, who was just two cells away. They allow him to talk to me now and then as they bring him back from his constitutional. 'He was alright the first few months I was here, by which I mean resigned. Resignation is the best state to be in when in jail. Those newspaper reports have disturbed his equilibrium. He is tense, almost frenetic; he would blow up the doors if he could, blow up the walls and get out. If the investigators say he is innocent, why can't his release be hurried through, that's what he seems to be saying and thinking about all the time. Sad case, needs sympathy.'

☛

The Jail grapevine is a pretty sure thing, and has the habit of turning out right. Abrar's orders from the court were on their way. But what can you say of people who jump the gun, or are impelled to jump the gun? Abrar felt almost forced into it. As it is his innocence was weighing heavy on him and one evening another inmate accosted him, picked up a fight and beat him up. If you are known as a 'terrorist', someone accused of planting a bomb that spat out shards, you are marked. Guys are itching to get at your throat. I was not there and the different versions are a bit of a blur. This much is certain that Abrar ran out through that forbidding stone corridor, and once out he made a beeline for the heavily bolted gate on the outer wall. Here the different versions fork away tangentially. According to one, the guard grappled with him and brought him to the Jailor. According to another the guard at the gate scurried into the sentry post and brought out his gun. Abrar pounced on the gun and held it against the man's chest. Later he tried to blow the lock, but the gun was not loaded!

He threw the gun and tried to climb the wall, but obviously failed. Old walls, high battlements, what can one do? The guards were loading their guns when the Jailor arrived on the scene, took command, got the searchlights switched on though it was still dusk, ordered the staff to see that the other inmates were securely locked in, and asked the guards to unload their guns. Then he began a dialogue with the man. 'Your release orders are here, Son, in my office, right here. Don't spoil things.' The two, I believe, could be heard hollering at each other.

'You don't believe me?'

'I don't.'

'Whom will you believe then?'

There was no answer. The Jailor sent for Father Baptista. Before the priest could come, he went into the office, and came out holding the paper. Then he started his long walk towards Abrar and showed him the paper. They talked for a few minutes and then walked back. In less than an hour Abrar was released from Jail. I have no idea why the staff sat on his release order for more than a day.

Next day I had a chat with the priest. 'The papers say the case against you is being withdrawn.'

'It should never have been lodged in the first place,' he answered.

'Looking forward to anything particular?'

'I told you... silence and greenery. I am not sure of the first now, because silence for me doesn't just mean lack of sound, there are other things to it. I am wary of clamour.'

'What do you mean? What sort of clamour ?'

'Doctor, I was also thinking of a different kind of noise—denigrating Gandhi, extolling Godse, the majority being asked to produce more children, the division of people into legitimate and illegitimate people. All this for me is clamour.'

Two days later the orders for his release arrived. Some of the lower staff had gathered around to pay their regards to him. I was surprised. Gaby was there and for once she was not hot under the collar, and even gave me a smile, a bit of a rarity. Father Baptista was wearing a shawl and had a walking stick on which he leaned a little. He looked like a swami as he walked out and I almost felt like bowing to him and touching his feet.

THE STORY OF THE SEMINAR

The seminar under the banner 'Whither Indian History,' misprinted as 'Withered Indian History' (the card was hastily replaced), was initially to take place in Rajasthan, Jaipur. It was the right place. But it had the wrong government, which didn't want any radical change in history as she was being taught. The All India Educational Council, if not moving heaven and earth, was certainly moving bulldozers to change the syllabi, and was asking historians to move their historical arses out of the board rooms and university senates and the All India Bureau of Historical Research. The director was a very powerful fellow because his entire family of seventeen members—sons, daughters-in-law, daughters, not forgetting the wife—a family unaccountably known to colleagues as 'the sundry seventeen,'—were all members of the All India Educational Council. The Council took recourse to whiteners and erasers in their initial revision of history. They erased the word 'beef' wherever they found it in relation to Vedic India and replaced it with 'mutton.' That was of course a triumph of sorts. They said that the Aryans never came from the North, but like *arhar ki dal* and *moong ki dal*, sprang from the soil itself. Guys who had got their PhDs on how the Aryans had crossed the Hindukush—whether in chappals or *khadaons*, barefoot or in rope sandals and whether they had eaten *sattu* or venison, or whether they had bitten into their cattle, were quite worked up. There were vague rumours that the Council would revoke their doctorates. An academic, his mouth a rictus of dogged fury, his face masked in a swirl of digital squares, said to Moon TV that he would rather part with his mistress than with his PhD. Hearing this on TV the mistress is said to have phoned her lawyer to file for divorce, but the lawyer told her to cool it, she couldn't get one.

The arguments of the minister, and hence of the All India Educational Council, were very logical. The Muslims came from Central Asia and West Asia, from Iran and Turan and what have you. The Syrian Christians had of course come from Syria and so were welcome to go back to Damascus or the Bekaa valley whenever they chose and the emigration stamp would be embossed on their passports without any bribes being accepted by officials of the Labour Ministry. It is the Buddhists, indigenous though they were, who betrayed the nation. That wretched Asoka spoilt it all by embracing Buddhism. Otherwise the Biharis would have kept thrashing the Odias, as they rightly did at Kalinga, and everything would have been hunky-dory. Now we were 'in this historical mess, this pot of glue, this jam jar infested with leftist flies, this pocked hide aswarm with secular fleas, this nest of wasps, this hive of bees which ate off our own indigenous Jamun tree and yet hummed its dissonance on the desert air'. The argument was so succinct, persuasive, so cut-and-dried, it was a logician's dream!

So the minister held a press conference and said let foreign indigents go from our land. His secretary whispered, No Sir! Use the term Indigenous Foreigners! '*Arre kya* phrase *mara hai*,' said the minister, 'most post-modern, *kya*!' So he said to these foreigners, 'We wish you well. You can have both our *vibhuti* and our *sahanubhuti* ["What linguistic *khubsoorti*!" exclaimed the secretary] May you travel abroad and go foreign. May you go to Syria or Lebanon, to Tyre or Sidon. May you get to these lands by sea, or to their seas by land. May you not get copped by the Copts or bruised by the Druze. May you alight on some gentle Alawite. May you not cringe before the fundamentalist fringe. May you eat *pakwan* at the hands of the Ikwan.' Then he looked up at the sky. 'But may they leave Bharat, hey Bhagwan!'

Even as Danjishaw was leaving for Jaipur a telegram arrived that the venue of the seminar had been changed to Guru Nanak Dev University at Amritsar. A friendly Akali government was ensconced in Punjab. He reached there and they took him to the University Guest House. No liquor shiquor here Sir, except vodka, they told him. 'And why do you allow vodka?' he asked, a bit puzzled. 'Because it looks like water, ji,' they said and laughed. Dan was careful and went without a drink that evening.

Next morning, Dr Gurmeet Singh Gill joined him for breakfast. Gurmeet was to preside over the first session, and in fact all sessions of the seminar. Danjishaw asked politely, 'Will you have some tea?'

'That is precisely what I don't want, ji,' was the answer.

'Coffee?'

'That is precisely what I don't want, ji. I will have lassi.'

The minister had not turned up. They waited for him for an hour by which time a message came that the great man would not be coming. But as the delegates were moving to the hall, they were ambushed by Moon TV. The great Barsaat Bhatt, who had become famous for her business chat show called 'Rialto Bytes,' was present in person to interview the delegates. She tried to get at Dan first but he said, 'Get off my back, will you, Luv,' and strode into the hall.

Gurmeet Singh was not so lucky—she cornered him, like a lioness that cuts off the retreat of a fawn. God had given Barsaat Bhatt both the gift of the gab and the gift of the flab.

'Dr Gurmeet Singh,' began the great TV personality, 'now that the minister is not coming, does that mean that your seminar has been sidelined? Does it imply that the historic decision to tinker with history textbooks has been consigned to the dustbin of history?'

'That means no such thing, ji. Seminars are for intellectuals, for an exchange of views. The coming-going of minister shinister is incidental, ji.'

'You mean the sinister minister, don't you?'

'That is precisely what I...' here the microphone failed, and Gurmeet Singh's 'don't mean ji' went unheard. It proved catastrophic. Barsaat Bhatt lunged once more like a lioness at her prey. 'You just heard Dr Gurmeet Singh talking of the sinister ministerial presence, which he and the seminar are now safe from. You can see the relief on his face, you can see his chest heave with the proverbial sigh of relief. The absence of the sinister minister, as Dr Gurmeet Singh so aptly termed it, will ensure a free and frank discussion on this seminal subject. Barsaat Bhatt with Chaya Hiranandani, Moon TV, Amritsar.'

The telecast cooked Dr Gurmeet Singh's goose. Within an hour he got his marching orders. Served by a police despatch rider, (this was Punjab after all) stating he had been suspended from service for drunk and disorderly conduct. He was put in a police jeep, and taken for a medical examination. The doctor opined that the learned Gurmeet Singh had at least half a gallon of booze in his belly, though all that the poor fellow had taken since morning was a glass of lassi. Seminars are so dull, said Danjishaw, while relating the incident at Ranikhet, that their appearance on the entertainment stage, however fleeting, needs to be welcomed.

A RUSSIAN STORY

As the out-of-work school master came out of his ramshackle tenement he saw the horse cart and the sorrel mare. (Was he the out-of-work master or was he the out-of-school student, thrown out because he couldn't pay the fees?) He observed the mare, as thin-legged as he had seen her last night. The nag in fact was so thin that the space between the shaft-bars of the cart looked half empty. The cart was huge, the bottom filled with firewood and on top of it a mound of hay held together by a thin coat of hessian, lashed with ropes. For a moment he did not dare to look up from the cart to the man who drove it, or rather was trying to drive it. Then his gaze lit on the man and he was shaken to his roots. It was the same barrel body, the same coarse, greasy face and grizzled beard he had seen in his dream. Same man and horse, only the cart was different, not filled with wine casks, but a hillock of hay. He shivered, though he was not sure whether the shivers were caused by the cold, his hunger, or the terrifying realisation that dream was turning to fact before his eyes.

Everything was still for that one moment, utterly still. Then reality broke upon him with a storm. A whirlwind of invectives was spouting from the cart owner's mouth. His whip kept crashing on the nag, her hind quarters and her neck. She gave a spasmodic jerk at each lash, her hoofs beat a tattoo on the cobble-stoned street, striking a spark once, but the cart stood immobile, just too heavy for the nag to nudge into any sort of forward movement. People had stopped walking on the street, and were laughing at the whole scene. The huckster himself, dressed in a sheepskin coat, weighed half a ton. A heavy woman was sitting beside him cracking walnuts and laughing. Some of the bystanders scowled at what was going on—was this fellow a Christian or a Hun, they asked in whispers.

The whip now started descending on the nag's head and eyes, just as in the dream. He had to put a stop to it. He wouldn't let him get hold of an axe and kill her, as had happened in the dream. He remembered the name of the fellow from the dream, but he didn't want to call out. He thought his mouth would be sullied by pronouncing it. He advanced towards him and shouted, 'This time I am not going to let you kill the mare!'

'This time!' the man asked bewildered. 'I've never killed her before!' He guffawed and almost lay back laughing. Some of the bystanders spluttered with laughter, some others didn't know how to react. He himself, the knight errant in ragged clothes and a hungry stomach, was not sure either. It had struck seven and he had urgent business at hand, in that little room with geraniums and yellowing wallpaper and muslin curtains that draped the window glass which had turned opaque with soot. Time was ticking away, he thought, and he had got himself into this. He knew it was irrational, an absolute eclipse of reason, but he couldn't withdraw now. Chaps would snicker. He had to take him on. 'I'll hit her on the eye,' the cart driver cried, 'stop me if you dare.'

How could he match a fellow twice as heavy and tough as himself? He realised the fellow could blow him away with one of his curses. He didn't trust himself to match him—the trouble was he didn't trust himself for most things; nor did the others. The one thing he could trust himself with was anger—anger against arrogance, deceit, greed, cruelty. Cruelty he could never stand nor understand. Seeing the man hitting the animal, hatred had followed anger in equal intensity, except that he didn't know whether he hated more the dream and the man in the dream, or the fellow in front, battering the thin legged mare. (Could one hate a dream? He had thought of that in a flash as he had set out for his evening enterprise). He was unsure if he felt more for this nag or the one axed in his dream. His mind may have been clouded, as always by a windstorm of thoughts, but his anger was focused.

That was the trouble with this thought-storm, he reflected. The brain got too crowded, often with the wrong things. Just when he should have been concentrating on the job at hand, making sure that the younger stepsister had left for her appointment, he had got waylaid by this hay cart, firewood cart and the drunk odious driver. He advanced towards the fellow. What if he used his whip? He could, he had a whip and was sitting pretty, at a level higher than his. If you are in a fight and hold a whip, you'd be foolish not to use it.

As the cart driver lashed at the mare and raised his arm once more our scruffy-bearded, hollow cheeked, out-of-school student made a grab for the whip. He got his hands to it and a tussle took place between the two. The cart owner was taken aback at first and the whip almost slipped out of his hand, but he leaned forward and got a good grip over it and pulled really hard. For a few seconds they tugged and strained at the whip. The student was clever. He suddenly let go off the whip and the owner slid back so heavily that he fell from the cart to the great amusement of the bystanders. He still clutched the whip in his hands though and walked up to the knight errant with great deliberation. After that it was pretty nasty business for the whip came down on the student a dozen times, on his back, his arms, his face. And the bully kicked him for good measure. The student felt the pain but his mind was still working away at the opportunity slipping out of his hands. Must be quarter to eight by now and the younger sister would be back at the house. What was he to do, he thought as he lay on the ground while the burly peasant was flailing away with the whip.

People were clustering around with a bit of concern now, but no one intervened. Then he saw the younger sister. She was so tall she would stand out even in a crowd of men. She was advancing timidly, pale as ever, uncertain. He saw the colour rush to her face. 'That will be enough, Oleg Kostyreva.' A silence followed. (Why were these silences un-spooling away, he caught himself thinking.) She was known to be so timid, people, those who knew her, were surprised. Speak like that, and to Oleg! She was timid as they come, this second sister. He knew it. Everyone did. She was dominated by her elder stepsister and beaten into the ground, though she was a good six inches taller. Even her own inconsequential business, buying and selling used household goods, she conducted only with the permission of Alyona Ivanovna, her ugly, avaricious stepsister. Lying on the ground, with the whipcord biting into his hand, (he had grabbed it once again) he was taking it all in, the past moving like a reel across his mind.

'Why was he coming between my horse and me? I do what I like with her, do you hear.'

Lying on the cobblestones, he heard. He couldn't answer, even if he wanted to. No sound could emerge from his throat, he realised fleetingly through a curtain of mist. He couldn't concentrate, there was a phalanx of faces in the crowd, he noticed. There was that perpetual drunk, trying desperately to keep his balance, eyeing him through his own personal fog. His 'high-born' wife was there too and his daughter by his first wife whom the high-born one had driven into prostitution. What a family! Why should they be here gazing at him as if he was some weird spectacle? His tired brain, his flogged body were trying to wrestle with too many problems at the same time. Problems? So where was the problem if some sordid family suddenly appeared on the balcony of his mind, but he realised that was too florid a way of putting it! Good God, how could he be thinking of things like that, lying on the road, and half the town gazing at him. He heard a cabbie shout at his restless horse and realised his own prone body had held up the traffic. The police could be coming shortly to remove him, so that people could move on to the Church of the Trinity or the Church of the Spilled Blood, or wherever they wanted to go, to buy tobacco or bread for all you know. Yes and what about the police, that contemptuous officer with the waxed moustache and the explosive temper, who thought it was an insult to look at him in his rags and his dishevelled hair and his scrofulous face? Was he here? He looked around. Thank God he didn't see him, and the rings on his fingers and his hair pomaded and slick and the gold chain snaking from his waistcoat pocket. Best to keep away from the fellow, he thought. He looked around at the crowd and the street and thought it was a still, like one of those Daguerre types that people were talking about, the aristocracy that is, not plebeians like him. But there was no law against hearing things, was there, even if one was hungry and down and out? Or could one perhaps define it as the stillness behind a bad painting—a red coat, soiled shoes, a cravat, greasy faced women, and behind the crowd a restless cab horse pawing away at the cobblestones and his abusive driver shouting at him to stand still.

'You can get up now, Rodion Romanovitch,' she said, the tall, gangling second sister. Her diffidence seemed to him to have returned. So had the pallid face and the hurt look which seldom left her. That was as it should be. People should be themselves, birth-marked with their characteristics, easily identifiable. He got up. That coiled spring energy of his had gone out of him—hunger and the beating had contributed to that. It was eight in the evening now, well beyond vesper time. The evening, till now, had been sicklied over with the pale cast of intention. He was blessed, thought the student Raskolnikov. The nag and the drunk owner and the younger sister had prevented him from murdering the pawn broker.

LOVE ACROSS THE SALT DESERT

The drought in Kutch had lasted for three successive years. Even when clouds were sighted they passed by, ignoring the stricken country. The monsoons had, so to speak, forgotten to land. The Rann lay like a paralysed monster, its back covered with scab and scar tissue and dried blister-skin. The earth had cracked and it looked as if chunks of it had been baked in a kiln and then embedded in the soil crust. Cattle became thin and emaciated. The oxen died. The camel alone survived comfortably, feeding on the *bawal*, camel thorn. Then one day the clouds rolled in like wineskins and the lightning crackled and the wineskins burst. Though two years have passed since the drought ended, everyone remembers that it first rained on the day when Fatimah entered the village. This is how she came.

What would he not do for her, the daughter of the spice-seller, she who smelt of cloves and cinnamon, whose laughter had the timbre of ankle bells, whose eyebrows were like black wisps of the night and whose hair was the night itself? For her he would have crossed swords with the devil! For her he would have become a heathen in case she had decided in a moment of perversity to only take a kafir in her arms! For her he would cross the salt desert!

He had stayed the day at Kala Doongar, a black hill capped with basalt, the highest in Kutch. He had set his camel, Allahrakha, free to crop on the *bawal* shrubs. At dusk he paid homage to the footprints of the Panchmai Pir on the hilltop. He left some food there and started beating on his thali, according to the custom here. In a few minutes jackals materialised and gobbled up the food. This was auspicious. If they had not turned up he would have considered the ill effects of the omen serious enough to have cancelled the journey. A lamp was lit in the Pir's honour every night on the hilltop and the flame could be seen all the way from Khavda. Over a hundred years earlier, Panchmai Pir had trudged these salt wastes serving the people, accompanied, as legend had it, by a jackal. Reclusive by habit, he used to retire to thorn jungles, where apart from his vulpine companions, none else dared to disturb him. The custom of feeding the jackals lingered since then.

Najab bowed before the flame and set out. He left behind the camel thorn shrubs and the area once famous for its savannahs of stunted grass, but now sere and brown as the desert. He had left behind all human habitation, Kuran being the last village. For the next three days he would not be seeing any *bhungas*, those one-room mud houses, circular at the base, but tapering into conical thatch roofs at the top. Now only the sandscapes stretched out before him, mile upon mile. Water splashed in the *chagals*. With the name of the Pir on his lips Najab Hussain set forth.

Najab's diffidence was notorious among his friends. He was known to have blushed at the mere mention of a girl. A smutty remark made in his presence almost gave him a touch of eczema. A strangely introverted lad with dreamy eyes, no one had ever associated him with any act of bravado. His father, Aftab, would say, 'All that my ancestors and I have acquired during a hundred years, this lad will squander away, not because he is a spendthrift but because he will be too shy to charge money for what he sells!'

He had crossed the Rann on four occasions earlier, though he had turned twenty only a month ago. But each time he had either accompanied his father or that wily old smuggler, Zaman, the veteran of a hundred illegal trips into Sind. Each time they had taken tendu leaf, worth about five hundred rupees, and sold it across the border for twelve hundred. But between the pay-off to officials and to the intermediaries who arranged the sale of the bidi leaf, to the man who took the camel out to graze and to the friend or relative who harboured them, there was precious little left. It was just enough to buy some used Terylene garments or cloves and then it was time to make the long trek back across the desert. It was during one of these trips that they had stayed with Kaley Shah, the clove-seller. 'He is a distant relative of your mother,' his father had told Najab. Kaley Shah was tall and well-fleshed and his thick-jowled face had a purple tinge about it as if somewhere along the way it had got stuck with a discoloured patch. He always wore a *tahmat* of black and white checks. Within a day Najab discovered that the fellow was an absolute rogue who drove such a cussed bargain that, for the first time in his hearing, his father started mouthing obscenities.

But his daughter Fatimah was a *hoor*, with eyes so bright that they would have lit up the darkness of the underworld. She was taken by this quiet, pleasant young man so ready with his smiles. But she could hardly elicit a word out of him. Fatimah had been under pressure to get engaged to someone in the village known for his slurred speech and grotesque stammer. Just my luck to run into mutes, she thought. But then, as she caught him staring at her, she laughed back. And in the evening when Fatimah repeated the performance and her face flooded with excitement, as if she dared him to take the next step, he had flung his arms around her in a reckless, dizzy moment. Yes, he would come again, he told her, and saw her start with disbelief, for he seemed to have answered her unarticulated question: would he come again? This time he would come alone with no father or uncle to cramp his style. And as he left he looked behind to find her gaze following him, her eyes like a pair of storm lanterns in the dark.

Ever since his return to Khavda, Najab had been straining to get away. What was there about the Rann that he did not know? He could cross the Rann in the daylight, leave alone starlight, a thing none of his elders had dared to do! 'You can't keep a randy buck on the leash,' his father Aftab had philosophised to his mother. And the next day he had gone and bought himself two maunds of tendu leaf used for bidi wrapping, and hence highly priced in Sind. And one morning Aftab was woken up by a shout from Zaman. What does the old rogue want, he muttered, rubbing his sleepy eyes. Zaman asked about Najab's whereabouts.

'The boy has been sulking of late, but he should be around. Anyway, what business is it of yours?' The old man could not hide his irritation.

'Whom are you trying to fool, Aftab Mian?' asked the smuggler. 'Don't you know that Allahrakha is also missing?' In these border villages the pattern of life was such that if a man was absent along with his camel, it was taken for granted that he had made a foray across the desert into Pakistan.

Aftab went into the mud enclosure where his camel was kept and found it empty. His heart sank. He ran into the house to see if the bundles of tendu leaf he had bought had been taken by the boy.

'Oh the fool! That son of a fool,' exclaimed Aftab, almost shaking with fury. 'He has forgotten to take the leaf with him!'

'Whom are you trying to fool with all this drama?' called out Zaman, who was still standing at the door. 'That son of yours is not as innocent as the world believes. He is a pig and the son of a pig.'

There was no limit to his chagrin. Zaman was the man who kept the Pakistani rangers across happy. Anyone crossing the Rann without his support was running the gauntlet with the law. And here this fledgling had blundered in without as much as a word to him, or a salaam or a hundred-rupee note! 'May Allah bring him safely out of this!' said the old rogue piously. He means just the opposite, thought Aftab. Nothing would please him more than to see Najab turned into carrion with vultures hovering around.

'Don't worry, Zaman, Allah will see him through!' he said testily and banged the door shut in the smuggler's face.

As Zaman stalked off, Aftab went in to break the news of their son's escapade to his wife. She would faint, he thought. He found her crouching with her back against the mud wall. She did not even blink in surprise. She just sat there cowering as if he had just slapped her and was about to do so again. Allah! She knew it! She knew it all the time! She was waist-deep in this conspiracy along with her son and never even breathed a word about it! His eye fell on her bare arm.

'Where is that gold bangle my father gave you, woman?'

'You need not worry. Najab will return with cloves.'

The long-striding Allahrakha kept a brisk pace. A strong south wind drove the tang of the Kori creek back into Najab's nostrils. He followed the stars, the Milky Way flaked with mica, the Great

Bear shambling towards the north. Before dawn he had reached his destination, for a sandy elevation palisaded with the bones of dead animals told him that he had arrived at Sarbela, over twenty miles from Kala Doongar. He was already beyond the international boundary. Here he rested. During daylight movement was impossible. The Indus Rangers would be looking from their bamboo watch towers. And in the heat everything became a mirage. A depression in the sand looked like a splash of water, a freak, stunted cactus gave the appearance of a grove and a camel looked like a huge prehistoric animal on the move. Any movement was sure to be noticed through binoculars. Otherwise too, the day was no time to venture out. For the hard flat surface of the Rann, littered with shingle and salt, turned loose and soft under the sun and the wind whipped it into the eyes.

When the sun came up Najab took his first drink of water from his *chagal*. At noon he had his first meal—dry, stale bread with onion. By now thoughts of Fatimah took a vicelike grip over him. An entire night lay between them, he thought. And the distance was less than ten miles! The thought of it made him writhe even as the sun started beating its hammer on the anvil of the desert. A whiff of the tangy south wind caught his nostrils again. But this time it brought with it a thin, dappled veil of cloud, patches of which lay overlapping like fish scales. Within an hour this corrugated cloud had covered a substantial portion of the sky, looking for all the world like a stretch of wind-rippled sand. Yes, this was the time! He got up and shook the sand from his turban. Even as he harnessed his camel he thought that Allahrakha was looking at him quizzically, as if asking what the hell he was up to. At one level of consciousness he knew that this was madness. He knew of overworked camels dying of fatigue, of the patrolling parties of the BSF and the Indus

Rangers, and the mirage-chequered, trackless wastes of the desert. But he succumbed to a rush of blood and the face of Fatimah beckoned him like a mirage.

Najab crossed the International Boundary Pillar No. 1066. He knew the track he had to take, bisecting the two posts of the Indus Rangers at Jagtarai and Vingoor. But he strayed ever so slightly, and from their watch tower they saw through their binoculars this sleek camel, warped and distorted by the heat shimmer into a lumbering leviathan. An Indian slipping into their territory with tendu leaf right under their noses, and that too without paying any hush money! They were not going to stand for it. Najab was in a trance now, events flashing past him like figures on a screen. The mile-long chase, the firing from behind, the spent bullets flopping in the sand and then the rising wind which churned the dust into his eyes and then rose between the hunter and the hunted. When the dust settled half an hour later he was alone in the Rann.

The next few hours passed in a daze. He was mortally scared that Allahrakha may die of fatigue. To ease him of his burden he now started walking beside him. Within an hour the salt had scraped the callus from his feet and scarred them with agonising cracks. Under a hot tin sky, the Rann was blazing now, throwing up white needles which hurt the eyes. And as the Rann palpitated, it haunted him with its mirages, pools of shadow, scooped half-moons of water. He wandered as if in a trance, attempting to lick the receding edges of the mirage. Then light thinning away, and an hour or two later, dusk, and a thin plume of smoke rising from a dung fire. Allah be praised! He was now within range.

He waited for night to descend and then struck out hobbling on his toes, for this desert odyssey had cost him his heels. Within an hour he was at the clove-seller's door.

Fatimah rose from her bed like a panic-stricken doe as he called out her name softly through the window bars. It took some anxious moments for it to sink in that it was Najab. Her lustrous eyes lit up the dark of the room as she opened the door. Thank God she has a room to herself, he thought. And later, thank God her bed doesn't creak!

After the gall, the honey, after the cactus sting, the feel of rose petals, after the scorching day, the waters of the night.

Two hours before dawn, Kaley Shah was woken up by the beat constable banging on the door. 'A smuggler has come across the Rann, Kaley Shah. You wouldn't know anything about him, would you?'

'*Kasam tumhari*, not a sparrow has entered the house or the village. Even the dogs have not been barking tonight.' Then he added with a knowing wink, 'Why should a smuggler come to me? What can I give him except some red chilli powder to carry in his backside!'

But the law was not amused. 'Kaley Shah,' he said sardonically, 'your belly is stuffed full with silver. It would outweigh even the dirt in your heart!'

The constable's words rattled like a sack of empty cans in his head and prevented him from sleeping.

'You have a guest,' said Fatimah as she brought him his tumbler of hot, steaming milk next morning. 'It is Najab. He stayed the night in the cattle shed.' For a moment he was terrified. A smuggler in the house, the police prowling all around and he did not even know of it! One would think he had been on ganja! His meeting with Najab had been brief. The wretched fellow had brought no tendu leaf.

'First you come unannounced, dragging the police behind you, and then I find you have come with nothing! Trading with you is going to be a dead loss, son, with the cops on your back and your hands empty.'

Najab thought that Kaley Shah's waist cloth, with its black and white checks, looked like a chess board. He would have to make his moves carefully. He showed the gold bracelet. 'I have come for cloves, chacha *jan*. And I shall pay in gold.'

The next two days Kaley Shah was busy buying cloves and arranging to get Allahrakha grazed a few miles away, by a cowherd. Otherwise the presence of a strange camel would have let loose a babble of tongues. Najab slept in the cattle shed in the evening and slipped into Fatimah's room late at night.

'They want me to marry Mahfuz Ali,' she told him. 'He is related to us from my mother's family. The way he stammers! You should hear him! His tongue just gets stuck on certain sounds, as if gum had been applied to half the letters of the alphabet. Urchins start mimicking him the moment they set eyes on him. It is just a step removed from being hounded like a madman and pelted with stones.'

'Has it never occurred to you to take a ride on Allahrakha across the Rann?' She had kept silent and silence was assent. It was as simple as that.

The first lurch of the camel next evening and they were off. He had waited with his camel at the outskirts of the village and she had slipped out after her father had started snoring. The moment was too big for them and they did not speak. It was only in passing that she thought of the village she was leaving for good. As for quitting one country and entering another, she never gave it a thought. Where did one have the time for Pakistan and Hindustan when one was eloping with one's love and crossing the desert which divided, both physically and symbolically, the two countries? For her it meant just a shift in dialect, a smear of Kutchi added and a little of Sindhi sandpapered away.

The camel lurched and bumped onwards and Najab drove him hard. By the time they reached Sarbela, Fatimah was exhausted and fell asleep.

She woke up in the afternoon to find the sky overcast. It turned ominous in the evening with depth upon depth of dark-edged nimbus gathering at the summons of a storm god. Another night they journeyed facing the wind which hurled the sand in their faces. As they neared Khavda, the thunder started rolling and reverberating across the skies.

Three times during the night Aftab had opened the door, thinking his son had come. But it was only the wind knocking against the door. This time the banging was persistent. When he unlatched the door he found Allahrakha shying away from a streak of lightning. Huge, isolated drops of rain were falling, kicking up the dust. Aftab steeled himself. He would not allow any relief, any expression of joy to show on his face.

'Son, have you brought anything?' he asked, an edge of iron deliberately introduced into his voice.

'Yes,' replied Najab, as he ushered Fatimah in.

The rain stormed down and swept away three years of drought.

TROJAN HORSE

The trouble with memory is that at times marginal recall is more difficult than total recall. Some people doubt if memory can be selective at all. Mother doesn't speak much, she only speaks when she is spoken to. That, as you can guess, doesn't make for much dialogue. And when she gets into one of her black moods, she digs herself into a coal pit. We have had these bouts on the subject of memory before and they have not led to much, except for dismay on her side and my astonishment at her dismay.

When Mother is in one of her dreamy moods she says things like, 'You can see the night in the rainwater there.'

'Where?' I don't know which puddle she means. In any case night is all around. One doesn't have to look for it in a rain puddle.

Or she says things like, 'Summer is lean this year.' I ask her what exactly she means and get a grudging answer. 'The vineyards haven't purpled as they should.'

One winter evening she nods westward. 'The light is as precious as gold.' It is not as if we have been discussing twilights and things earlier. Again, she breaks one of her crystal silences with a weird statement, 'I have witnessed sacrifices and thought that flames consecrated. Now I know they only burn, dispossess.' Consecrate what? Burn what? 'Everything,' she snorts back. She is in the habit of producing such staccato statements out of nowhere and then lapsing into her familiar silences.

If memory is twilight, one city framed against it is as much a silhouette as another. If I left her city when so young she shouldn't be expecting those graphic recalls, your memory swinging, as it were, on each loose hinge of the city gate. And how do you recall a rolling plain? Can anyone memorise meadow flowers, for heaven's sake? Or roads and ruts and grass verges? Hills perhaps, if they are distinct enough. And vineyards draped over the hills. Beyond this I am not about to concede anything. I can be as stubborn as mother. Same genes, you know.

'Can you remember nothing at all?' Dismay already etched on her face, nostrils flaring with barely suppressed anger… 'Not even the watch towers, the battlements?' No, no, no. How often do I have to tell her?

It is not the differences in age alone which make her brusque with me. She has never once thought I have reached her mental level. Moreover, she always says she has seen so much that it can fill a hundred lives. So where does the question of a prolonged conversation arise? I've seen so little. If your memories stampede you on to the edge of a precipice, you should either live away from cliffs, or cauterise your memories. But who'd tell Mother that?

Some nights are quick with a multitude of dreams. Some nights are aflame with a recurrent one—watch fires all around on a vast endless plain. Then things afloat on water—ships perhaps, stealing on to the beach, and later fire and noise. That's the dream, more or less. The sequence changes sometimes and fire-noise precedes the ships. The day I finally confide in Mother, I remember how the morning has settled here, the poplars leafing, moss stamped on the roots of a cypress tree, the scent of rain arriving before the rain. I tell her of the watch fires on the plains, of fire and incredible noise, and of boats moving in.

'That's no dream. That's memory!' snorts Mother.

A few days later she opens up. She thinks it is necessary now that I can't be kept in such a state of innocence (or did she say ignorance?) all my life. 'High-throned' Jove ordered who was to die in battle the next day; 'Cloud-Compeller' Jove, who decided when a cloud would suddenly rain darkness on the field so that his son's corpse could be spirited away for lustration and embalmment. Die like a man but get embalmed like a god—that was Sarpedon's fate, Mother would say.

We drift down with the summer, past Pergamum, past Phoecaea. It is another thing that one summer may have overtaken another during this slow drift, as we oscillate between coast and hinterland, scrub and pasture.

Wretched as we are, I can't remember being happier ever. As I look back, this is the time I wake up to memory. Mother's heartburns are not mine, not as yet. I am not bothered about what we've left behind, not just gates and battlements, but myth-memory, the nexus between sin and destruction, dire prophecy and fulfilment, this web spun out of intangibles—hubris and divine wrath and heroes foredoomed. And those small stories scribbled on the margins, say Xanthus, the horse of Achilles, prophesying his master's death.

My troubles come in the shape of a tall man sitting astride a big chestnut horse. He has just one eye, and watching it I stand transfixed. It is this half a moment that takes a terrible toll on me. He wants only me. He doesn't want mother. I am aghast. I expect mother to protest and lash around the way she used to sometimes when particularly painful memories buzzed around her. Instead she just eyes me with a sort of icy compassion. It is I who leap and scream as I am led away while she looks on sorrowfully.

The weather couldn't have been more beautiful, the wind a caress, the sky a dream-blue. The day couldn't have been more auspicious. It is the seventh of the Delphian spring month, *Bysios*, the birthday of Apollo. My fate couldn't have been more scurvy. One-Eye takes me to the plaza. It is the weekly market day. People have come to buy everything from pots and pans to scythe and hammer, from oil to amphorae. As if there had never been a war. I even hear laughter. People swarm so close around me, I can smell their sweat glands and their appetites. I can sense the penumbra of their admiration around me. A slave squats in front and examines hoof and fetlock. Others laugh.

'There's nothing to investigate here, son. He's perfect! A talent of gold for him, a talent of gold!'

A man steps forward, a Carian by his looks. 'I'll buy him. Where's he from?'

'Lycia.'

'Doesn't seem from those parts. I am from Lycia,' says a teenage boy grappling with the first shoots of his fuzzy beard.

'What do you think a Lycian horse should look like—your twin brother?'

People guffaw. The teenager scowls at One-Eye, takes a step forward and gives me the once over. 'He's been branded.' People press around me further but can't read my burn-mark. An old man is called in. He hobbles up to me and examines the mark from all angles.

'It says Polydorus.'

'Polydorus?' people look at each other.

'Yes, Polydorus, son of Priam. Slain by Achilles the day he killed Hector.'

A cold silence suddenly drips down, as if from a giant icicle. People suddenly turn on One-Eye.

'From Troy is it? And you tried palming him off on us?' A man catches One-Eye by his shirt and shakes him so you hear his glass eye rattle in its socket. And right in the middle of the plaza One-Eye is roughed up.

It is the same story at other places. People say with a toss of their heads, 'A Trojan horse indeed! As if we haven't troubles of our own!'

One-Eye later takes it out on me. 'Because of you I can't sell the rest of the bloody herd.' He has Assyrian horses, Akkadian horses (You can tell them by the smell) and even horses from the desert, brought by people wearing outlandish dresses, with robes as big as tents, and the backs of their necks covered with cloth that flaps when they ride.

'I'll have to pay someone to buy you, pig,' says One-Eye as he starts whipping me in a frenzy. I don't even neigh in protest. I want to be as faithful as a dog. But a reputation for loyalty is a bit difficult to establish if you are a Trojan horse.

The man who takes me in is Euphemus. He has high cheekbones and raffish hair that falls like black silk over the nape of his neck. He seems to be surrounded by swirls of laughter. That's why he is such a favourite with the girls, I discover later. Barely a week after he has bought me, he notices an open window overlooking the street we are passing through. A lovely woman stands there combing her hair. He at once turns round, proceeds to the house, and opens the gate. I hear my hooves ring on the cobblestones in the yard. After keeping us waiting the lady opens the door.

'Yes?'

'I've come to sell horses.'

'Where are they?' I can feel Euphemus fidget in the saddle. 'Well, to begin with, there's the one I am riding.' They both laugh, I don't for the life of me know why.

'Why don't you come some other day? There's no one at home to discuss horses with you.'

'That's precisely why I want to come in now.'

And he suddenly leaps from my back, and she laughs as he enters the house closing the door behind him. No one has even bothered to tether me. I nibble at a few measly grass shoots sprouting between the flagstones, drink some water at the fountain, and litter the yard. Boredom moves my bowels as nothing can.

In less than an hour he is out and we canter off. The next day we come here in the afternoon, and again he says he wants to sell horses and again he enters the house with her to discuss the sale. Else, why should he waste another hour?

But a week later we troop in with four other horses. This time the men folk are there, three brothers, all mean-looking and muscular. Their huge, blubbery father is also there. I feel I can handle him, but there are many horses I know whose spines would cave in under his weight. Much as Euphemus tries to sell the horses he does not succeed. They want ME. Euphemus coughs a little and tells them I am from Troy. What on earth for, I wouldn't know. Never mind, say the brothers, we'll pay you less now. But its him we want. Euphemus obviously wants a better price.

'If Achilles had ridden him, he'd have still been alive. He would have out-paced the arrow.'

Euphemus can say the weirdest things. The father does react. His belly rumbles with laughter, but his face remains stoic, I notice. The girl, standing behind, tinkles like a silver bell. The brothers frown at her and she goes in, closing the door reluctantly behind her.

Better horses than I have been exchanged for smaller pieces of silver. So who am I to complain? I settle in with my new masters.

Euphemus is not seen for the rest of the summer. He has gone foraging for more horses, more trade. With the onset of winter, on a slightly chilly day I see him coming in again, this time on a black mount, which he seems to have brought from Lycia. He tries the same gambit. 'I have another horse to sell,' he says gravely, and then breaks into laughter. She chimes back, keeping the door open for him.

I notice the mood in the house darkening. The brothers have always looked glassy-eyed. But these days there is an extra coldness about their gaze, which makes me uneasy. The eyelash hardly flickers over the eye now. There are arguments with the girl and one day she is even beaten. Things don't seem to be looking up.

I leave Smyrna dismayed and terrified by my passion for Ilione. I camp around pools with my horses. It is summer still, the light overwhelming, burning the water as it falls on it. I miss that horse from Troy—so young and frisky with quicksilver hooves and a leap that could match a leopard's. Its whinny could put an entire valley on edge. I had been buying and selling horses as a child, since the time I had taken to the road with my father, some twenty years back. But I've never seen anything so perfect—beauty, speed and spirit all rolled into one. I had to sell him for the woman, Ilione. There was no other way getting round her brothers.

I can't make up my mind whether this is good luck or bad. But there has to be a strong dose of destiny to all this. A day earlier I had bought this horse, the finest I have known. And as I pass through the street, this window flies open and framed there stands the most beautiful woman you could think of. There is a shimmer to her long brown hair which she combs with steady strokes. The horse turns round on his own. I don't have to give the slightest hint with the reins. It's a corner house with a fountain in the yard. She takes her time opening the door as she combs her hair and fixes it in a coil at the back of her head. The moment I tell her that I've come to sell horses, she sees through my subterfuge. It is the most disbelieving smile she flings at me and yet the brightest and the pearliest I've seen for a long time. And when she says come some other day, there's no one to discuss the deal, I know exactly what she means and move in.

Her laughter is so gentle and there is such compassion in her hands. Also in her eyes. I have never been looked at that way, never been handled thus. This is the place for me. Who wants to get stuck in Mysia, so far up north, with the murderous Hellenes so close, and Troy still smelling like meat being roasted over a hunter's fire.

Going around isn't pleasant anymore. The smoke from Troy seems to fill the skies. In my own native Mysia, people are still sorry about the fate of our hero, Eurypylus, who died fighting alongside the Trojans. My relatives in Pergamum can hardly talk of anything else. A few months on the road, and I seem to have had enough. Why must the body be under attack constantly, and tendon and muscle be bruised and torn week after week? Why must one smell of horses all the time? The tug of Ilione gets stronger as winter is about to set in. Memory is moored to her. Seated on a black horse I had bought recently from the desert tribes, and with two other horses in tow, I turn around and set out for Smyrna.

The first day of my return is like the first day I saw her, the one window open, the knock on the door, the males absent. The Trojan horse whinnies when he sees me. I visit her every second day. I just can't wait. I send word through some elders to Ilione's father that I want to marry her. I get myself invited for lunch.

There is a cutting edge to the cold that day, the wind sullen, the sea cold with currents of the far north, currents which carry with them memories of ice. The grilles on the facade of the house seem prominent, and their shadows move in with me into the corridor leading from the front door. Even when I take a seat in the room I notice the floor is stippled with the shadows of these thin rounded bars. The brothers are there, as vitreous-eyed as ever. They seem to be looking into space even when they are looking at you.

'You seem to be familiar with the room.'

'Incorrect,' I answer. 'You never let me in when I sold you the horse, remember?'

The father intervenes. 'This is an oblong room, as you can see. People show surprise when they first come in, that's why he asked.'

I don't believe what he says.

'A horse trader moves through half the world. If he is surprised at every turn of the road he would die of perpetual astonishment.' I make it sound like a reprimand. (My brother once told me I speak to men as I speak to horses. Wrong. I am much gentler with horses). I want to break the ice, and add, 'How's the horse?'

'The wooden horse you've smuggled in to capture your Troy?'

I would have expected someone to laugh. No one does. They don't even seem to smile.

'I don't take the easy way out or the easy way in. The world would be a sad place, if we all looked for wooden horses to get to our individual Troys.'

I feel I have made that little speech with a certain aplomb. The viands and the wine appear. Ilione does not.

The brothers are in and out of the room too often. They never seem to settle down. A half hour seems to go by in small talk and watching their agitated traffic to the kitchen and sometimes to Ilione's room, and back. Then suddenly I hear a visceral scream from the very entrails of Hades; an underworld scream that seems to have travelled half the world, through half a dozen nightmares and demonic spells to reach me. It is the Trojan horse screaming repeatedly. Instinctively, I feel that something terrible is going to overtake us, that some black shaft, with death riding on it, has left the bowstring of destiny. (I may be forgiven this ornate language, but at this moment of heightened awareness, nothing else would suffice.)

An irresistible urge catapults me from my seat. I rush to the front, and not a moment too soon, for at that precise moment the brothers emerge from the kitchen, their faces twisted and their knives gleaming. They chase me through the corridor, calling me horse thief and shouting obscenities. I dash to the front, my shirt, ripped up from the back by a slashing knife. The horse, which has raced to the front, and was bucking and rearing but a moment ago, now stands still as if begging me to mount. My black horse from the desert stands tethered. The gate is bolted and there is no time to open it, for the brothers are within yards of me. I jump on his back and with one unbelievable bound he sails clear off the low wall and gallops away.

☛

My black mount from the desert has been returned to me through a slave of the brothers. They, in turn, refuse to take back the Trojan horse.

A month hasn't passed since he took that flying jump over the low wall. But he is bad business. People first want to buy him. Once they know where he is from, they won't even touch the others.

I also notice the burgeoning of a skin problem with him, a brownish discolouration spreading across the white patch of his belly and his ribs.

What I have learnt from gossip and Ilione's neighbours doesn't surprise me. The brothers have gone around saying various things about me. 'He circles the house like a shadow; he enters the house like a thief.'

There is nothing like a murderous chase by three knife-wielding thugs to change your perspectives on romance. Distance sets in like a season—winter this time. Now that the knives are out, I might as well go. Smyrna suddenly loses its appeal. The dust and the scent of the road call. And I leave my regrets behind—the women with the compassionate hands and the long shimmer in her light brown hair and a high vaulting mettlesome horse that flew over a wall.

☛

Euphemus has left. I browse in the meadows and stand under a tree at night to keep off the frost. The sea is in revolt against its confines; the smell of salt all-pervasive. The wind from the sea has a knife to it. Talking of knives, I saw three of them being sharpened in the backyard that day. Then Euphemus came over and I started feeling uneasy. It's when the brothers took the three knives that I understood what they were for and I screamed and bolted to the front.

With nothing much to do now, I give myself over to dreams. Sometimes I see One-Eye waiting for me at the end of a valley of rose-coloured shale, right at the spot from where the pasture begins to stretch. Like a hunter at a salt lick. I think of retreating into the valley even though it had shed its last vestiges of green a million years ago. But I am slow to move. A prolonged ennui spreads from the spine down to my hooves and I know I will not be able to go back. Returning to valleys you have left behind is always difficult.

I feel stiff, as if my limbs are calcifying. A tight feeling has gripped my ribcage, to go along with a change in colour there, like a belt mark that has been around a bit too long. Slowly the colour and the marks have dug in, brown as timber, and with the grain of old wood.

Euphemus had left. I said that before, I thought. I spend my days browsing in the meadows and standing under a tree at night so that the frost doesn't descend on me. Dreams also descend like frost, and I see Mother, shaggy and mournful as ever and old and shrivelled as a raisin in those hazy visuals that film the eyes during sleep. At times she is frantic with worry.

'Do you remember that dream?'

'You mean that dream about fire and all the rest?'

'Yes! What else would I mean! Well hang on to it. Don't let it disappear ever. Do you understand? It is very precious.'

And sometimes she starts giving homilies. As always she is enigmatic.

'There can never be an escape from what has happened. Don't try to get rid of it or wish it away. Live with the past, it's a nice thing to live with.'

A HOUSE IN RANIKHET

Her father had died in the malarial foothills. Sadly enough, not through bullets, or shrapnel or a landmine—the preferred modes of death during the War. He had died of high fever, as it frothed its way to delirium and death. She had come now, fifty years later to see if her forgotten childhood would come alive in some mysterious way she couldn't define.

She was a bit run-down and wracked with asthma. As long as she had the money, her holidays were quite unlike this one. She would take the hovercraft at night (the night ferry was always cheaper) to Ostend. She had a friend who lived, of all places, in Bruges. She had been mesmerised during her first visit to the postcard city—the quarters for the crusader's wives or widows, and the medieval enclosure that quarantined the plague-stricken. Could anything have been more romantic, she had exclaimed, as her friend had stared at her a trifle baffled.

'There's nothing romantic about plague, Cynthia, for Chrissake.'

But people die, and so did her friend in Bruges. And each death leaves the near ones a bit older. Cynthia had felt lonelier as the days went by. And so at long last this desire to see her father's resting place before she found one for herself. Graveyards peg memory and sentiment to place, site. And visiting them has very little to do with flowers or a short prayer. You want to be with yourself for an hour or two. Just you and your thoughts about the person interred. Yet, at the end of it all you fall into the usual trap—a photograph of the cemetery—flowers, weeds and all, and a close-up of the headstone with its slightly archaic language. And just as well that the language should be a bit old. Esperanto wouldn't do here, would it? She felt resentful that her mother had got nothing engraved for her father. Just the name and the regiment and the two dates. Others had written rather florid things about their dead. A lady's headstone surmounted by seraphs, proclaimed that 'beauty of sentiment, majesty of wisdom and the grace of persuasion ever hung upon her lips. The bonds of life being gradually dissolved, she winged her flight from this world in expectation of a better, this day the 15th January 1896. Her afflicted and affectionate sister Maria (undecipherable) in full assurance of their final reunion.'

Why couldn't her mother have got something written like that? And after one lingering look at the slightly dilapidated cemetery and the unmowed grass and a ten-rupee tip to the wizened caretaker, she had taken a bus to Ranikhet. She was there in two hours, a little shaken by the sharp curves the bus driver took while joking and chatting when he should have been concentrating on the wheel. And she had fallen in love with the place—the quiet October afternoon, the arc of snow peaks struggling to keep their heads above the ascending clouds; oak on the higher ridges, and every now and then an old cedar that dwarfed everything else. Old cottages with their red-tiled roofs. And the silence, above everything else, punctuated every now and then by a gust of breeze through the pines, with the yellow needles drizzling down.

She got into a small hotel owned by a silver-haired Bengali lady, Mrs Ganguly. She ordered an omelette for lunch, not wishing to risk the curry. In the evening when she sat on the hotel terrace, drinking her tea and watching the dusk change colours, the Bengali lady suggested she go inside or she could catch a chill. She dined alone at night—a tepid vegetable soup of sorts, lamb cutlets and a slightly fiery tomato gravy followed by a solitary mini mound of caramel custard.

She got friendly with the landlady in the next few days and once over coffee mentioned her asthma. We have a homoeopath called Tripathi here, the landlady told her and directed her to a cottage called the Pine View. His success rate with asthma cases was very high. There was no harm in trying him out, she thought. At least she would have an excuse for visiting someone.

So a week later she found herself in Pine View, though she noticed that much of the pine on the opposite hill had been reduced to charred stumps in a fire. On the higher ridge though, you could see the oak. They should call it Oak View now, she thought.

Mr Tripathi's dispensary was basically one room and a garage. Little translucent plastic bottles peppered with little white globules lined his shelves. Tripathi was wearing a thick brown khadi kurta and woollen churidars. A light grey stubble sat inconspicuously over his pale skin. He had a mane of thick black hair that flowed back and added ballast to a thin mousey face. He sported a phallic ashen mark on his forehead. Why people in this country turned the forehead into a canvas for all manner of artistic and geometric designs, she didn't know. And she didn't want to know either. Would be too abstruse for me in any case, she thought.

The smile on Tripathi's face turned slightly ingratiating when he saw Cynthia. A white woman was a rarity here. He was polite. He took her pulse, asked her about her history, her family history, what brought on the wheezing, her reactions to cold and dust, and how she felt when the seasons turned. Then he sent a chit to the garage and back came a plastic bottle with those little white pellets. Every six hours she was supposed to take six of those globules but without ever touching them with her fingers. What chemical properties could be destroyed through contact with her palm, she failed to grasp.

'I may try these when I go back to Delhi. Here I am feeling fine in any case.'

'The town itself is a doctor,' said Tripathi. His laughter was so shrill that she reacted to it as to a hypodermic needle. But she liked the vibes here and the medicine did her good.

Two months later she came back to Ranikhet, a little before Christmas. The trees looked a little frosted and the ground felt hard as cement. Log fires crackled in Mrs Ganguly's lounge. Mrs Ganguly saw to it that Cynthia was served her dinner in the lounge itself right next to the fire. Everyone was surprised she was back. Some thought she had gone bonkers. 'You've come here in December, Mrs Cynthia Craig!' She had to correct people about three times before they learnt to address her as Miss and not Missis. There was a big block in the Indian mind, she thought, which prevented people from addressing any woman above thirty as 'Miss.' To the hierarchical Indian way of thinking a Miss ranked lower than a married lady.

'Yes, I've come here in December, as you observed so perceptively. It's so pleasant, so lovely.'

She went to Tripathi, now moving around in a brown balaclava cap. Why had she come here in winter? That's the trouble about the Indian, he is so predictable, she thought. She loved it here, rain or winter. Who wouldn't like to live here, she asked. The snow view at dawn, the early sun and the brilliant haze; the high cloud smothering the snow peaks in the afternoon, the rise of the wind and its abeyance; a lone cicada or two at dusk; a small drink and then dinner, with coffee near the log fire, to follow. Winter was a lovely word here. Could life be more wonderful than this?

'If you are that much in love with the place you must live here, Missis Craig. You must get yourself a house.'

'I am on the lookout for one.'

House-hunting was not easy. People were reluctant to let them out on rent. Why? Renting property out made more sense than keeping caretakers to look after empty bat-infested houses. As for selling property, people wouldn't dream of it. You must be out of your mind to suggest such a thing Ma'am, their looks seemed to say. She kept discussing her housing problems with Tripathi—a homoeopath does become a confidant and a counsellor of sorts, a position which an allopath would find himself uncomfortable in. Moreover, businesslike, as always, a doctor would have examined three patients in that time, made three times the money and prescribed an overdose of antibiotics to the lot of them. A homoeopath talks and talks, thinking all the while that he is ferreting out some hidden secrets of the patient's body through fairly meaningless conversation.

One day Tripathi could not resist saying that if it was a house she was after, and so desperately at that, he could offer her his own.

What did the fellow exactly mean, she wondered.

'Are you offering me Pine View for sale?'

'The very same,' said Tripathi, smiling animatedly.

'And what will you do?' she asked.

'I will go to the plains. I find it cold here, very cold. In the winters, I mean.'

As she got up to leave she asked if she should continue with the medicine. 'The same, the same,' he answered.

That evening she asked Mrs Ganguly what she thought of Baijnath Tripathi.

'Why do you ask?'

'Nothing special. But if one runs across a person a number of times one would like to know a few things—his reputation, his standing in the community, things like that.'

Mrs Ganguly thought that Cynthia was being evasive. She saw no reason to be too specific while answering a casual query.

'Well, he came here ten years back. He's a good homoeopath. Earns enough to keep body and soul together, and I believe he has got a law degree now, through correspondence or something.'

She mentioned the last bit with a curl of her lip. His family had never been up in Ranikhet and no one had any idea what they were like, she added. But there was no woman in his life, as far as she knew.

'Why do you have to mention women?' asked Cynthia, laughing. 'I wasn't about to marry him, if that's what you think.'

Mrs Ganguly appeared horrified. 'Hey Ram, what a thing to say. Perish the thought.'

There was a touch of mildew and fungus to Mrs Ganguly's English, thought Cynthia, and wondered why she hadn't noticed this earlier.

Barely a week later she was at Pine View once again.

'Tell me, Mr Tripathi, you were serious about the house, weren't you? You were not in your cups or something?'

Cups? Tripathi didn't understand. She noticed his face break into a rash of incomprehension.

'I was hoping you hadn't had one too many.'

'Shiva, Shiva! I have never gone even near to alcohol, Madam. Alcohol is sin. *Mahapaap*. Cow-meat-like.' He touched his ear lobes. She put him at ease, told him it was only a joke.

'Not a good joke, Madam!'

'Just a way of putting things across.' What she meant was she was surprised at the offer. She then sprang the question. 'How much?'

'How much what, Madam? I am not understanding.'

'How much for the house?'

Tripathi dropped his head, half smiling, half blushing. '*Ab aap sey kya kahen*?'

She had to remind him that she didn't understand Hindustani.

'What can I say to you?' Baijnath Tripathi dutifully translated, still blushing away.

'You'd better say it!'

Even to herself she sounded a bit desperate now. After some persuasion he mentioned a figure around two and a half lakhs. She tried to bring him down to four thousand pounds. 'I don't understand the Indian rupee,' she said.

'Oh really, Madam,' mimicked Tripathi, rather cheekily.

In any case it was fifty-four rupees to a pound, so what was he cribbing about, she asked. They struck a bargain.

The papers? she asked. He was an old hand at law, he told her. He would have the papers sent to her at the hotel. No appearance in court or before a Registrar—no nothing. Just give him a few days to have the papers ready.

A fortnight later, after a quick visit to Delhi and converting her pounds to the rupee which still stood or rather wallowed, at fifty-four to the sterling, the deal was through. Tripathi sent her some forms in Hindi and asked her to sign at a place or two. That was it. She marvelled at her luck. Four thousand pounds would be four months' rent in South London—Croydon or Dulwich. In sleazy Camberwell perhaps she could have stayed eight months on that kind of money. Here she was getting property for the same amount.

Tripathi moved out. He apologised for a locked cupboard, belonging to a previous tenant, he was leaving behind. And that was it. Cynthia enjoyed the winter and hoped there wouldn't be too many tourists in the summer. Winter was lovely, except for the nagging worry that summer may bring in tourists—especially the ones who ate chickpeas and chaat and carried transistors.

A maid came looking for some memsahib with a name that had something to do with bottles and she shooed her off. She took a trip to Delhi every six months or so to replenish her book supply. She had turned into an avid reader of novels and everything was grist to her mill, from Perry Mason to Milan Kundera. She pottered around the garden, though in summer Ranikhet dried up and the watering of lawns became a punishable offence. A beehive kept her busy—it took her six months to get hold of a chap who would smoke the bees out. And all she got out of it was one bottle of thick honey with the specific gravity of congealing wax. But the rains were lovely, the afternoons cool, the roads washed clean and the far hills speckled with mist, even though the peaks, the massive trident called Trishul and Nanda Ghunti and the rest were never visible.

And late in the second summer of her stay there, Cynthia heard a car rattle up the driveway. She came out to investigate, just as a rather buxom lady, in a peach coloured chiffon saree, squeezed herself out of the car.

They looked at each other in surprise.

'Nathoo!' shouted the lady in the peach coloured chiffon.

'There is no one by that name here!'

'What! Where's the chowkidar?'

'There isn't one!'

'And where is the mouse?'

'Who?'

'Tripathi.'

'He went back to the plains over a year back. In fact I bought this place off him.'

'You what? It wasn't his to sell. I just loaned him the garage to run his clinic.'

'He sold me the house!'

'The house! My name is Mrs Batlibhoy. I own the place and my father owned it before me. We were here before the War.'

She plonked herself down on one of the cane chairs lying in the veranda.

'You poor dear!' said Mrs Freny Batlibhoy. 'That little bastard seems to have done you in.'

'We are talking of the same person, aren't we?'

Freny Batlibhoy, slightly wide of hip and bulging of breasts, took a deep breath. She was trying to be as patient as possible.

'Thin fellow, looked as if he had just been hatched from a lizard egg?'

Cynthia laughed, despite herself.

'Long hair, mousey face, wore khadi? Has to be the same guy. There was no other Tripathi here ever.'

Cynthia was struggling against hope now. 'The lawyer. We are talking of the lawyer, aren't we?'

'Lawyer! Fraud *kethey no*! Sorry for breaking into Gujarati, dear. He was what they call a munshi here. A petition-writer at the courts.'

There was nothing much to say now.

'I am Cynthia Craig.'

She held out a limp hand which Freny shook vigorously. 'You stay as long as you like here. You'll be company. And we'll sure as hell sort that fellow out. Meanwhile, I hope my cupboard is still there.'

'O, is that yours?'

Freny walked up to the cupboard, fished out her keys from the handbag, and opened it. It was a cupboard made of walnut wood and was beautifully carved. She surveyed with satisfaction her sarees wrapped in muslin. They had not been attacked by moth or weevil.

'At least he didn't run away with my sarees.'

It was clear to Cynthia now. That maid who had come looking for the memsahib. The electricity bills which occasionally still came in her name. Cynthia had remonstrated once and they had apologised and rectified the error. That should have set her thinking. How naive could she be!

Freny summoned her lawyer and berated him roundly for letting Cynthia get swindled by that so and so. Eighteen months she had lived in this house. Couldn't he have warned her? Then she stormed into the police station. When she finished Cynthia's story the sub-inspector told her that the police station had already completed its quota of First Information Reports, or FIRs as they are known, for the month of June. 'And if you were swindled eighteen months ago, you should have come here eighteen months ago.'

'But eighteen months ago I didn't know I had been swindled.'

'Madam *kya*? Everyone know house belong to Freny Madam. If you had asked your servant girl, she would have told you. Two year you stay in house and you don't know who it belong? *Kya baat kartey ho*?'

By now Freny had worked herself into a rage.

'I'll complain to the District Magistrate. And I will write to every District Magistrate not just in this state but in every district of the cow or the buffalo belt or whatever you call it. I'll smoke that Tripathi out of his rat-hole.'

She started writing to everybody—Governors, Chief Ministers, District Magistrates. Meanwhile lots of things had happened. Elections had 'happened' and social engineering had become, if one could put it that way, a very lucrative avenue of employment. Freny started explaining to Cynthia what this social engineering was about. 'You see, the screws have become the screwdrivers and they are out to screw the others. You get it?'

Cynthia got it.

'And they have kept some of these derelict specimens of the loftier castes, just to make their government look representative—you know a socially comprehensive facade.'

Cynthia, poor girl, did not comprehend, but nodded her head nonetheless.

'I must explain this social engineering in greater detail some day when we have the time. But in short you must understand the nuts and bolts of the revolution. Well, the nuts have bolted and are seated with the board of directors.'

Even as she finished speaking, Freny knew she had said something stupid. But that is not how Cynthia saw it.

'That fits. That's revolution! Lenin couldn't have asked for more.'

Freny gave her a long, cold stare for once.

Neither from the high-ups nor from the low-downs have we received any reply, said Freny in despair one day. Since the authorities had remained silent as the sphinx (not that when they are noisy, the authorities are any less enigmatic) Freny and Cynthia decided to go to Lucknow to complain.

Home minister? There was no home minister, they said. They used the word '*Grah* Mantri *ji*.' Why? Has a *grahan* (eclipse) got hold of the *Grah Mantralaya*, asked Freny, coining one of her silly puns as usual. The babus didn't understand this aggressive Parsi lady with her quiet vilayati escort. The Chief Minister now looks after the Home portfolio, along with sixteen other portfolios, they told her.

'Must be a very busy man, your Chief Minister,' said Cynthia.

'Busy counter-intriguing, Madam.'

'Oh, is the opposition then smelling blood?'

'No, Madam, it is his coalition partners who are smelling blood. Other things also keep the *Mukhya* Mantri *ji* busy, meeting *mulakatis*, visitors or callers, and cutting ribbons.'

'Cutting ribbons?'

'Both immediately before and after elections it is ribbon time. Scissors are much in demand.'

I wish I could get within two feet of him with a pair of really long scissors, thought Freny Batlibhoy. But once he scented their problem, the official gave them some good advice.

'Why don't you see the Minister for Justice?' Freny thought her prayers had been answered.

'Do they have a Minister for Justice?' she asked ecstatically. She was told that the minister was out on tour but she could meet the deputy minister. They walked through the cluttered corridors swarming with people. Seeing a white woman and another who spoke in *Bambaiya* Hindi, the peon summoned the assistant of the Deputy Minister. He asked the ladies to write their names down on slips of paper. When they were handed over to him he mulled over the chits and said, 'With names like Craig and Batlibhoy you are not going to be called in. If one of you were a Miss Gangwar or Miss Jaiswal, it would have been different.' He asked the peon to step aside and suggested they knock and barge in.

Good fellow.

☛

They knocked and barged into a large teak panelled room, humming with six air conditioners. They advanced towards the corner where, behind a large glass-topped table, sat a thin man with a small triangular face and a mane of thick black hair.

'Tripathi?' asked a rather shocked Freny Batlibhoy.

The deputy minister took off his steel rimmed reading glasses to take a better look at the intruders.

'Baiju? Baijnath Tripathi?'

'The same!'

'*Saalo Chor*! The bloody thief! The same Tripathi who sold my house to Cynthia Craig?'

'The very same!'

He left his chair and advanced towards Freny, his face wreathed in smiles, his arms outstretched. Freny couldn't help enveloping the fellow in her arms and giving him an affectionate hug.

CROSSROADS

Nasreen

The maulvi is here, and I can't for the life of me think why. But of course! A month has passed, and he should be here, shouldn't he? That is, if Jamal wants to go ahead with all this. And Jamal *would* want to go ahead. He wouldn't be Jamal if he didn't.

And if the maulvi is here, the others would be trickling in. A little sheepish perhaps, avoiding eye contact. Some would get—they did last time—positively shamefaced and start looking down at my feet. That generally makes me very self-conscious about my feet. Toe-nails, rather. I'm glad they are unvarnished at the moment. And who is going to prevent me from saying anything I like? Not the maulvi, in any case. It is red toe-nails that make me feel uncomfortably aware of my feet.

Yet it was all about pigments. My self-consciousness was nailed to a scale of red. When the toe-nails were painted a mocha brown, I was less bothered. Still less, when they were pink. And if the paint didn't know whether it was mother-of-pearl or flesh pink, then it was just too bad. I could not care less. I was as self-assured as the most arrogant male.

When Jamal had stopped stroking my smooth instep, about six months ago, I knew something had changed. But not everything surely. So much for that ballyhooed female intuition.

The drawing room is so large that four long-poled ceiling fans hang from the high-roofed room, and when the fans whir with extra speed because of the aberrant voltage, the rods themselves start swaying. In the middle of the room there is an arch, which psychologically divides the room into the male half and the zenana half, although no curtain was ever draped along the arch since I came into the house.

More people are trickling in, like beads of sweat running down the armpit, wetting the bra strap and latticing the blouse with their salty stripes.

The maulvi's son has also come. He is mute. His lolling tongue hangs around the mouth, groping for words, which somehow never fasten on to it. The father brings him when he comes to read from the Holy Book during a Koran Khwani. I always have sweets and sherbet served and have taken special care of the boy. The father is always formal and correct with me. His hands never come up to his beard when he talks to me. With others he's always scratching his bristly goatee as if searching for body lice. When I offered him money once—very respectfully, mind you, with the chunni draped over my head and the money held in my right palm, with the left palm tucked under it—he declined. 'Give it to the poor,' he said. Saqina tells me later that I should have told him, 'That's why I'm giving it to you.' (The only female gibes about maulvis that I have heard are invariably delivered behind their backs). I have always noticed, with just a tinge of envy, how smarmily he greets Jamal, especially when my husband takes out his wallet from his sherwani.

The mind can wander even when under severe pressure and the eye swivels with it. Through the glass door I cannot help noticing a lizard sunning itself in the verandah. Beyond it, the eye takes in the red dots on the hibiscus hedge, looking from this distance like fireflies. Then I sense Zain Maami fluttering around like an old hen. I know she has been looking desperately for a spittoon. But I am in no mood to help anyone. Let them fend for themselves.

'Think it over, Jamal Mian! Think it over! Nothing is going to come out of this haste.' A moment later she gargles. 'Don't forget what I have just said. You will repent!'

Her mouth is stuffed with betel, and awash with sepia drool. She says this loudly, so that I can hear her clearly and be grateful ever afterwards. I could not be bothered. In my present mood I'm not sure what exactly I care for. Zain Maami is a do-gooder and like all others of this ilk, you are confronted with a mask here and something different behind the mask. She has never disliked me, but in the kind of trough I find myself in I would not like to take a bet on that.

Achchu Mian comes in, preceded by his cough, and sits himself down on the floor without once looking my way. Munney Mian, our neighbour, follows in jeans and T-shirt, the folds of his belly hanging over his jeans. He too doesn't look my way. Nanhey Mian, Jamal's younger brother, on the other hand, looks pointedly, even dramatically at me, salaams with head inclined, his fingers coming right up to the forehead, and then sits down. But most of the others give the impression of being positively frightened to look me in the eye. I am not twenty-eight yet, but even my shadow would make them jump today.

Daadi, that is the sister of Jamal's grandmother, comes and sits with me. Jamal's real grandmother is known as Daadi Amma. It must be hard on these old women, I think for an instant. They can't all be seen squatting with Jamal. And if they all home towards me they could easily be called hypocrites. I don't know how the word *munafiq* comes to mind: it doesn't just mean a hypocrite but also implies treason towards Islam. Just shows how foul my mood is.

My father was fond of hunting and metaphors of the hunt. He once told me a tribal saying he had picked up during shikar. 'When the arrow hits the doe, flies throng to the wound.' Why do I think of this now, at this rather crowded moment?

Daadi has been eyeing my midriff rather closely this past month. Is she noticing a bulge? I almost laugh to myself. During my periods of anxiety I have always eaten more. I always grew wider during my exams. After my MA in Sociology it took me a good three months to get back into shape. It was only after my waistline had shrunk that Ammi allowed me to be paraded before Jamal and his family and the wedding day settled.

And of course there is Saqina, her presence wrapping me and my days here like a shawl. She comes in early and Jamal almost bars her way, leaning a little, his arms spanning the doorway.

'And what do you want?'

'I want to see Nasreen.'

'And why do you want to see Nasreen?'

'That is none of your business.'

She almost has to force her way in. I have a feel for vibes. Who hasn't? Every vibe that comes from Saqina today feels right. There have been times when I have suspected her. It can be the way one laughs or just a glint in the eye, or the passing whiff of an odour that had disappeared ages back, which at times makes one woman suspect another. Then facts intervened. For eighteen months, or was it two years? But today she is beyond suspicion, her face clouded with emotion, enhancing her beauty.

With me things are different. They have to be. The face is unpainted, unpowdered, unrouged, and yet the lines of pain creased away. Sorrow has to be discreet. I have already put a ban on tears.

Jamal is building up pressure, turning the knob on tension to slowly break this woman. Or so I think.

Some cold water is served in trays, the glasses frosting with moisture. It is not the day for sherbet. The maulvi starts with Bismillah-ar-Rehman-ar-Rahim. He talks of Jamaluddin and the family and its 'high position' in the area. He talks of a time when affection suddenly sours and minds don't meet. He intones something in Arabic, which I can't understand, nor anyone in the gathering, for that matter. Then he suddenly keeps quiet and looks at Jamal.

'Talaq!'

But this time Jamal's pronouncement doesn't echo and re-echo like a gunshot, as it did a month earlier. In fact the word gets smothered in his larynx and there are some who have not been able to hear him. It is Achchu Mian, I think, who says, 'Speak louder.' I see, as in slow motion, the maulvi's restraining arm go up, but Jamal hasn't seen it.

'Talaq,' he says louder this time, so that he can be heard clearly. I see, again in sepia-tinted slow motion, appalled faces, half-horrified faces turn to the maulvi.

'This is irrevocable. The Koran makes it so. We all heard Jamaluddin Mian pronounce the word 'Talaq' a month earlier. And he has uttered it twice just now in the hearing of the whole majlis. What has been said now cannot be withdrawn.'

There is a big murmur in the room. Some people remonstrate. Daadi and Daadi Amma both look distraught. Jamal is still, head bowed, looking at the floor. I get up and am surprised that I can find my voice.

'I do not belong to this house anymore. I am leaving.'

I don't know if my ears are playing tricks with me but I can swear that I hear a sort of collective sigh, like air wheezing out through a giant air cushion.

☛

Two nights later at my father's house in Nizamuddin, I unpack the box of my memories.

'Are you really going to Hardoi?' my friends had asked.

'Which is the nearest railway station?'

'Does it have cabs?'

'And auto rickshaws?'

'Just tongas and horse-dung roads, perhaps?'

'You mean horse-cart roads.'

'I mean roads where the green dung steams and wafts away to glory.'

'Ameena!' They carry their hands to their noses. Ameena likes saying such things. She is (or was) a literature student and lays great store by what she considers realism.

'Never mind the dung. A buggy is what I want to ride in. And he has six servants! And a dozen mango orchards!'

'Half a servant per orchard?'

That has to be Ameena again. Is she envious, I catch myself wondering, and am ashamed at the thought. Why must thoughts shame anyone? Words, yes, actions, certainly. But the mind is just a passage, isn't it? And if a black bat of a thought wanders in and flaps around, what on earth can you do? Anyway, his orchards have impressed the others. They positively squeal.

'Is he handsome?'

'You will see him at the nikah.'

Actually, he is delicate-featured, with just the hint of a hollow cheek, and he is slight of frame so that I really want to hug him hard.

My father hires a canopy bigger than an entire hotel. A hundred bell-shaped chandeliers hang down from the canvas ceiling. Some glitter less than the others, because they are flecked with dust. There must have been half a ton of marigolds adorning every nook and corner of the wedding pandal, except where the nikah takes place, that is. This portion has been kept austere. The *Qaazi* doesn't like flowers. Dinner is out in the open, the entire area sprayed with barbecue kiosks. Prawn or fish, chicken or kabab, or diced bits of lamb, there is nothing that is not sizzling round a glowering spit.

When I move into that large, sprawling house in Hardoi, distance shrinks. The women in the household are spread over three generations of the family tree. Jamal has a sister, an aunt and two grandmothers of sorts. That sounds formidable. There is no other male. That is infinitely worse. Nanhey Mian, Jamal's younger brother, looks after the lands in Sandilla. Achchu Mian is a manager in a hardboard factory in Sitapur. I nod my way into marriage and my husband's family.

The lawns are more weed than turf, and there are patches without grass. The fountain doesn't work. The hedge is unkempt and tattered. In the kitchen the tumblers smell of roaches. At night an occasional rat clangs and rumbles through the vessels. The kitchen is soot black, with charcoal still feeding the *choola*. The two old ladies still drink water from the clay pitcher, while the fridge lies almost unused.

Yet it's fun in its own way. I get the lawns re-dug and have the hedge uprooted and hibiscus planted there. The winters are splendid. The thick molasses-like smell of the cane crushers, and jaggery, its smell, touch and taste all similar and of a piece, sticky and cloying, and blood-warm and sweet, as if by some miracle all senses have been reduced to the same scale. The cane-loaded bullock carts trundling on the road, raising puffs of dust that hang in the cold evening air. Returning from Jamal's fields after dusk we often encounter jackals, their eyes gleaming in the headlights like miniature sodium flares. And the lone mornings in the verandah—everyone else would be sleeping—where I read the morning paper—the *Pioneer* and *National Herald*. The Delhi papers come only in the evening. My letters home start slowing down, after an initial burst. Now and then a reprimand from my mother shakes me out of this total immersion in my new surroundings. I have not started on my thesis, for which I had registered with such keenness. All that seems to be moving into oblivion like a fading sound track.

Nowhere does this happen except in an Indian marriage—the way the present shears off from the past.

Jamal's laughter and his slim body are a thrill. A year slides by so quickly, I can't believe it.

Slowly Saqina enters our lives. She has been in and out of the house much before I came. She is, what you call, dynamic, buys and sells. Pottery from Khurja, hand-printed sarees from Farrukhabad, brassware from Moradabad, carpets from Badhoi. She sells not only to various emporia in Delhi, but even to customers abroad. She turns old printing blocks into exotic furniture. Business and travel have put her in another league. She is a cut above these other landowners who won't let go of their old, outdated lifestyles.

Jamal starts moving out of the house oftener now. Formerly it was a problem making him budge. On two occasions, when I thought he had gone to sort out some land problems regarding share croppers with the Tehsildar, I chance upon him at Saqina's furniture shop. During dinner, I let drop casually. 'Saqina is becoming a part of our lives, isn't she?'

'In this day and age, who isn't a part of whose life? Tell me that.'

He does it well, sounding even more casual than I. It is just two years since we married. Is he getting bored with me already?

One night after we made love I asked him, 'Do you know, one fine day what I half expect to hear from you while you climax?' He doesn't answer but stares enquiringly.

'Saqina!'

Jamal goes into one of those 'chee chee chee' routines adulterous Indian husbands and wives so easily break into when confronted by their outraged spouses.

I toy with the idea of taking a break and going off to Delhi. But one goes home when on top, which means with husband in tow and a baby forked on your hip. You can't just go off and wet your mother's chunni with some sob stuff about some more attractive girl having put your husband's heart in her pocket, or wherever such women place the hearts of those they have seduced!

After an initial drop into depression, I settle into a trough. Jamal is more courteous and solicitous than ever. (How do I tell the fellow it is not courtesy I want?) Sometimes I no doubt catch him giving me a regretful, yearning look. Or almost. And now and then I see, when catching him off guard, strange shadows ghosting across his eyes.

Before Saqina had trespassed into our lives (did she really trespass or had we left the door ajar?) I had pulled out my papers once and taken another look at the rough draft of my thesis. What are you working on, Jamal had asked.

'Passis.'

'Passis?'

'That's what I said.'

He seemed utterly bewildered. Why I should be tinkering around with such people was beyond him. I had felt contrite. My thesis was on 'The Not-So Criminal Tribes of India.'

'Does that make sense now?'

It didn't from the looks of it. But he knew a Block Development Officer who was a Passi. Dharamvir Passi to be exact. Jamal was bent on introducing us, and true to his word he brought him home one day, tall, wearing an incongruent golf cap at a rakish angle and a close-collar coat of Almora wool. He was a postgraduate. His English sounded like wood being chopped but his Urdu was suave and he could trot out a couplet from Zauq or Mir at the drop of a hat. When we got round to talking about his caste he said, 'We Rajpassis are a lazy people. We were actually called Rajbansi, of royal lineage, but after a while (read a few centuries or so) we fell out with royalty. Some took to their cots and were called Khatiks. Rajpassis sprang from a Passi woman who married a Rajput king of Pathaungarh. But that could be a lie.'

'It most probably is. Isn't it remarkable, that castes a rung lower always have a woman who has slept with a Raja, pardon my saying so. That's how genealogies get manufactured. But no one talks of a Bhil, Baheliya or Khatik sleeping with a Rajput princess.'

I find him eyeing me clinically, admiration and surprise written all over his face. We met again, you bet. One goes to the Block for seed, fertiliser, the works. Since Jamal is either lazing in bed or venting his spleen on the servants or visiting Saqina, I decide to take the jeep out. Dharamvir always has interesting titbits. 'There are other variations of that Khatik story. Each region has its own legend. The Pratapgarh one credits the Passis fighting a great battle against the Raja of Mewar. Some of them fled and hid behind a cot and so were called Khatiks.'

That is nonsense, and I let him have it. He just shrugs. I am surprised to find that when neatly dressed, he can almost look handsome. Next time we meet, he wears a herring-bone tweed and brown slacks and a shirt unbuttoned at the top so that one notices his lighter tone under the neck. I dislike his two-toned shoes, though and tactlessly let him know what I think of them.

'You don't like them. I will never wear them again.' Such a trusting childlike look he gives me. (Now that I think of it, was he dissembling?) Without noticing it I find the barriers between us giving way. Not that there is any dearth of barriers in our country. A man-woman relationship is like a bloody obstacle course. That goes for even half-innocent relationships, for come on, there are no fully innocent relationships.

He looks down at my feet.

'Where do you buy such sandals? Bombay? No wonder. One never gets to see such lovely sandals here—or feet.'

I get self-conscious about my toenails but force myself not to look down.

'Arre. Madam, you are blushing.' (The word he uses is *surkh* to denote the colour flooding my cheeks.) And that too because of your feet! What happens when people compliment you on your face?'

I want to tell him it is none of his bloody business, but restrain myself. (Restraint comes with female genes in our country). Let it be I say. I hope I am not sending any wrong signals. We have been strolling in his office lawn. I admire his roses, he is really good at them. How he manages to rear roses that are black—there is certainly more noir than rouge to them—beats me. I buy seed and drive back.

A surprise awaits me at dinner. 'You'll have to get busier on the land from now on. Buy yourself a nice pair of ankle-high boots so that you can actually walk in the fields. I suggest the Chinese at Hazrat Ganj—Hong Chu, I think.'

'And what will my dear husband be doing while his wife is busy with plough and sickle?' What will prevent him from moving his arse? I don't ask that of course, a husband's arse is out of bounds in Hardoi.

'You can be sarcastic.'

I want to tell him I am not being half as sarcastic as I want to be.

'Well, you'll be happy to know that I have entered into business. So I won't be able to spare too much time for...' he lets the sentence hang in the air.

'Business? What sort? Are you going into diamonds, or will it be bullion, Jamal?'

'Furniture.'

'Oh, so a joint venture with Saqina, is it? I see.'

He had used the phrase 'entered into,' hadn't he? Freudian slips can't be pointed out to husbands.

I don't toss about at night. The moment I hit the bed, I nod off as if I was on sleeping tablets. Sleep itself is like an empty cavern. Not one stray *bhooli-bhatki* dream to bother me. Only on waking I don't feel refreshed. And the mirror talks of dark rims under the eyes.

☛

The next time the BDO comes to the house he brings rose plants, and gets them planted at the right spots. Later we have coffee out in the garden. I am alone, Jamal having left for the furniture shop. The mali too has left after planting what Dharamvir had brought. I veer the conversation his way. 'Why were the British so prejudiced against certain castes and tribes? Why were some of them labelled "criminal"?'

He laughs. 'The British did us no wrong. They even established reformatory schools. They were fed information by the Brahmins and the Thakurs. They were told we were thieves.'

'And were you?'

'Well, we were pretty good at it, thievery and that sort of thing. There was certainly a hereditary tag to it. Legend tells us that a devotee of Brahma, Kuphal by name, was told by Brahma to ask a boon. He demanded that he should become perfect in the art of thieving. The boon was granted. There is a saying among us that the very mention of the name Kuphal acts as a mantra for thieves and removes all fear from their hearts.'

We both laugh.

'Of course there is an antidote. If you mention the names of the wives—Maya (illusion), Nidra (sleep) and Mohini (enchantment), the thieves are never successful.'

When winter ends, of course, we can't sit out in the sun. Each time we enter a doorway he asks me to lead, and his arm comes to rest on my back momentarily, as he sort of propels me forward. I like being propelled. I almost find it exciting, this proximity to male strength. Our arms brush against each other and I don't draw back.

But despair gets blacker. At night a block of hard ice sits upon my heart. That is the trouble with narrations. You talk of highs on a graph, a visit here, a clinch there. But the cellular texture of daily life never gets reflected. That stream of feeling, which stays with you and keeps on flowing, even if it is merely recirculating around you, hardly ever manages to speak. It can converse only with itself. When I try to articulate it, words get in the way.

And one day he brings up the talk of Kuphal again. Outside it is so dark that dusk seems to have descended early. He knows all about *amavas*, moonless nights, and that sort of thing. His right arm has propelled me into the drawing room and towards the corner where we have a yard-long swing.

'Tonight the name of Kuphal would be on the prayer beads of some thieves.' It is an attempt at banter from my side.

'Don't you think we ought to be taking his name today?'

'Are we on a thieving spree?'

'Aren't we?' and he draws me towards him.

Saqina

She turned bloodless. I had never seen blood desert a face like this. The cheeks took on the off-white tone of blotting paper. Her eyes were bloodshot, though. If I had my way I would have hugged Nasreen and cried. Or I would have taken a stick and bashed Jamal's head in. Nasreen got up, rock steady, and said with extreme dignity that she didn't belong to the house anymore and was quitting, or things to that effect. They could get stuffed. She didn't say that, but you can bet the phrase crossed her mind.

I never thought her capable of such dignity. And such courage. In two days she chucked it all up and walked out. Back to Nizamuddin. No tears, no scenes, no shouting, nothing. Packing her things quietly. The voice normal; forced to be normal. You may have detected some strain there, some indication of effort, but I noticed none. She must have placed great store by normality. Even her appetite was the same, two scoops of rice, one roti, some dal and a vegetable. She refused to touch meat now. What is more, she carried her plate to her bedroom. Only I ate with her. Those two days I was her family.

At least tell your people, I kept coaxing her. This will come as a terrible shock. Think of them! Nasreen never got in touch with them till just three hours before the train left. She didn't want her parents rushing over to patch things up. There was nothing left to patch up, she said.

She gave back all the jewellery to Daadi Amma, all, that is, that had been given by Jamal's family… returned even the presents. She took away whatever was hers. Marriages, deaths, both end up with the carving up of estates. I am becoming profound!

Daadi wanted her to keep the presents. Nasreen wouldn't hear of it. Easy and matter-of-fact. No dramatics. Everything normal. Except for a glacial look one caught by accident, and the black ice in the heart which supplied that chill to her eyes.

I said something earlier about being profound, didn't I? Profundities don't come easy when you have broken up a marriage. When Jamal first started hurling himself at me (metaphorically, the physical bit started later) I gave him what was coming to him.

'You have a wife, Jamal.'

'But it's you I find attractive.'

'One doesn't always get what one finds attractive.'

'I do.'

'Not this time. And wipe that silly smile from off your face.' The trouble with Jamal was he wasn't easily deterred. You need a lot of steel in you to repel repeated advances from someone with Jamal's looks, his boyish face and tousled hair. I deal with timber, wood carving, printing blocks. Not steel.

'It is just two years since you married, Jamal,' was my constant refrain. I kept him away, though each time I looked at him I wanted to rummage through his hair. Sheathed in a silk kurta as he always was, his slender frame cried out to be hugged. I could break his ribs, I thought, if I ever put my arms around them. 'Please God! keep him away!' As things turned out, Jamal's first embrace was so fierce that it was my ribs which were in danger. I had to struggle for breath. It felt great. I never brought up that just-two-years-since-matrimony routine again.

We were happy, but a small town has its restrictions. Where could one meet except at the shop? We took trips to Lucknow, Jamal driving me in his jeep. Though we were fairly uninhibited, there were of course tensions. (And I would think of her often, five and a half feet of longing all draped and covered and forgotten in wifehood.)

His constant presence at the shop was irksome, though. He would slouch around the whole day. I had work to do. I was importing printing blocks from Farrukhabad where they were used for printing designs and motifs on cloth and sarees. One day he dumped a bag on my table, and said rather loudly, 'We are in business from now on.'

'Haven't we been in business for quite some time now?' I whispered conspiratorially. He emptied his bag on the table, fifty thousand in currency notes. I stared at him.

'This is sheer vulgarity.'

'Vulgarity? And what do you think we have been up to for quite some time?'

He actually mimicked me, the bastard!

'Get out!'

'Don't be silly, Saqina. I want to join you as a partner, as your financier. I have no expertise. The least I can bring in is money. That also gives me an excuse to be around.'

'You bastard,' I said laughing loudly, slipping obediently into his arms. A fortnight later he had told Nasreen.

'What did you say to her?'

'She'd better start working. Buy ankle-high boots so that she could supervise work on the land. She tried to be sarcastic. "What will my dear husband be doing while the wife is hoeing and harvesting?" That kind of stuff, you know. I was so furious.'

'Is that all? I would have said, "And why won't my husband move his arse while the wife is slogging in the fields?"'

'Wives don't say such things.'

'You mean mistresses can?'

He did not choose to answer. After a few minutes he resumed. 'I was going into business, I told her. She immediately knew I was joining you.'

That soured my mood for a week. That week I didn't let Jamal come near me.

After a few months he started mentioning the BDO. It never registered with me. After all, I was working, touring. Somewhere the word got stuck. The next time he mentioned the BDO I sat up.

'What is this about the BDO? What is he to you?'

He was nothing to Jamal, but he was visiting Nasreen. I laughed.

'So bloody what?'

He gave me a hard stare. 'The fellow is a Passi.'

So that was it, caste. 'You don't expect this Passi fellow to do any hanky-panky, do you?'

Jamal got up and lit a cigarette.

'Anything can happen in matters of the heart. You had been around for as long as I know. How do you explain this… this sudden passion for you, this spell… ?'

'Spell?' I was a bit bewildered.

'The spell you cast over me… I speak in metaphor, of course.'

'Of course!'

'For two years after my wedding I resisted you, you may not know it.'

This was a revelation. He had actually shown character for two full years! 'That's all very fine, Jamal. You give in to a whim of the loins, and call it a matter of the heart.'

Withering look. It took me a while to mollify him. Over the next few days I drew the story out of him in snatches—it was not a thing he liked to talk about—how this Passi fellow came and sat in the afternoons, on the plea of bringing in rose plants, or a coleus pot. A dozen ashoka trees had been planted along his boundary wall! The fellow must be spending money.

'But there are servants around.' It was half statement, half question.

'Yes, but that is terrible, isn't it, the servants watching the Begum talking to a *gair*, an outsider.'

I had never heard him use such phrases before. Begum, outsider, they looked like words he had suddenly imported from his ancestral past. After some beating around the bush, he came back to the subject.

'Some of these bastards disappear in the afternoon. They want their siesta, if you please! There are times when, I'm sure, there's no one around.'

I half expected to see fire erupting from his mouth and broke into uncontrollable laughter.

'Do you want the servants there or don't you? Make up your mind.'

For the best part of two years I kept telling him to spend some time with her. She needed companionship. He would always nod his head and never do a thing about it. Things changed dramatically. Anything dramatic has to happen all of a sudden. I found him muttering to himself, one evening, tense and just a little haggard. 'She went to a picture with the Passi!' he screamed. It was a slap on his face, he said. She did it just to humiliate him! Some people look positively ugly in their anger, their facial muscles pinched and tight, and their jawbones working away. Jamal looked positively handsome in his rage. I let him rant and curse. There was little point trying to make him see reason. I had the shutters of my shop downed, saw Jamal to his car and went home.

A week later I realised that people had been cold to me of late. Kamil, a lawyer friend, gave me the brush off. My cousin Naseem looked through me as we passed each other on the street. What was wrong? Jamal hardly made an appearance at the shop, and when he did come in, he was gone before one could corner him. I asked my shop attendant what Jamal was up to. Sahib was engaged in *salah mashwara*, consultations, I was told. (Trust Urdu to use two words where one would do.) Then he casually let drop, in a voice that was barely audible, that these days Jamal Mian had been busy with the maulvi. The maulvi? What on earth for? He read my thought.

'Maybe Sahib is getting religious.' He said this with a straight face.

The man was getting ready for divorce! I threw fits, I pleaded with him, I told him I wouldn't see his face if he went through with this. Jamal remained stone-eyed and stone-faced. Don't make a fool of yourself. The whole town will laugh at you, I told him. As if it hasn't been laughing at me while all this tamasha was going on, he said bitterly, trying to emulate some wronged thespian he had seen in some movie. Possibly Dilip Kumar.

'I will have nothing to do with this, or with you. Understand that well, Jamal.'

He nodded, but I don't think he ever understood. Within a few days I returned all the money that he had brought in, threw his things out and slammed the door in his face. It was him pleading now. 'Don't do this to me, Saqina! Not at this juncture!' But I had done it, and I never go back on what I do.

A day later I phoned Nasreen. What's happening? I asked. What a dissembling little bitch, she may have thought, I would have, were I in her place. All she said was, 'Why don't you ask Jamal?'

'I can't. I've thrown him out.'

During those depressing weeks, I was with Nasreen every other evening. (I may be exaggerating, though). I did all the talking, waiting in vain for some confidences from her side to sideslip into the conversation. She never really opened up, as if all that was personal and really intimate about her had been locked up.

☛

Nasreen

Passengers, porters, parents. I am crowded with questions which I deflect, as best as I can. Abba looks well, despite his salt-and-pepper stubble and his eyes a little pinched with anxiety. Ammi asks me nothing and engages in small talk in the car. The rain is cold and the tyres hiss, especially when we negotiate the roundabouts. As we circle round the turquoise-domed Sabz Burj at the very threshold of Nizamuddin, father asks for possibly the sixth time, 'Things are all right?'

'Not so good.' I answer.

There is no point going over all this again. Parents have to be shocked when their daughters are divorced, or they wouldn't be parents. There will be exclamations (from the mother) and much gasping (also from the mother). Lower down the social scale there would be breast-beating. This happens when there is more than one woman in the house. (Fortunately my mausi isn't around. Just wait till the two sisters meet. There's going to be much surreptitious weeping, I know.) And still further down in the slums, cooking fires would not have been lit in the whole lane, obscenities galore would have been exchanged, and people may have reached for their staves and their axes.

Fortunately our *choola* is lit, for I'm feeling hungry within an hour. Mother is a shade disappointed by my undiscriminating appetite. To feel hungry at such a catastrophic moment is nothing but vulgar, her look seems to suggest. Mother's chunni is already wet, what with wiping her eyes.

Recriminations, of course, there are in plenty as time goes by. Why didn't I tell them earlier? Why could I not drop a line secretly? (There was no need of secrecy, Abba, I could have moved wherever I wanted. I could have written in their presence and they would have posted the letter. They are not that kind of people.) Then what kind of people are they? Parents can get difficult. Of course they could have sorted the whole thing out. Ammi, what could you have done, cajoled, begged, grovelled? Just as well you didn't come!

But she keeps rummaging in my past. Her questions are insistent, extending even to my sex life with Jamal. I am short and laconic in my answers. A bit unfair, I agree. I still don't know whether Ammi was ever able to get what she wanted—to ferret out the kernel of meaning from the husk of event.

At dusk, the familiar smells of Delhi drift into the room, that amalgam of diesel fume and smoke from burnt leaves which the cold keeps at eye level. The mist cowers in the wings. In the morning it will turn into a ground-fog. I am home.

It takes Ammi two days to notice that slight bulge in the belly. A number of questions circle round me like anxious crones.

'There's nothing Ammi, lay off!'

The first bout of nausea strikes within a week, a restless feeling that rises to the throat and slowly subsides, but never completely. Each upsurge is stronger than the previous one, forcing the belly, as it were, to move towards the gullet, till after hours of ebb and flow I finally throw up through both mouth and nostril. Later I recline against the bed-rest. Father comes and just sits there, without saying a word, just sits there watching, perhaps hoping to catch some fleeting reflection drifting across the mirror of my mind.

Ammi can't believe I have no regrets. Sometimes I can't believe that either. They think my life is in shambles. I don't. Logic must take a backseat sometimes. In four years one found love and one lost it. Love was a frontier and one had crossed it. Just once perhaps, but so what? That was enough. And the final break was clean. Thank God I have been spared those endless quarrels—the re-enacted, recurrent ending of love.

Terrors, of course, are always around. But the moment they show up on your face, you've had it. They will swarm all around you and you will be lost in the whirlpool. Saqina was frank enough. Even the two nights she stayed with me she thought something would snap within me, perhaps I would start crying and thrashing around in my dreams. She expected the ice to mumble and moan, as it cracked beneath the shroud of sleep. In fact, it was she who started babbling away, and I had to shake her up to bring her out of that rapid-fire burst of incoherencies.

I think of her often. I even wrote a short letter, a one-page affair, rather awkward and parchment-stiff. Ammi tore it up the moment she scanned through it. 'Divorcees shouldn't write thank you notes to the other woman,' she said disapprovingly.

My terrors remain voiceless. They are centred around Jamal. Suppose he wants me back! Suppose he walks in and falls on his knees, or does whatever errant husbands do when they want their just-booted-out wives back in the house?

The nuances of the season change. The late evening sun now pours through the window, the light stippled as it floods in through the grille.

The child in the belly has already started speaking to me. His is the language of touch, and he tongues me with it. He has been there for over three months now, being baked brown in the oven-heat of my belly.

His face is downturned and his face is upturned as he floats in the waters of my womb. The seed rehearses its destiny all the time, every moment.

He is big. He is all over my belly; growing bigger by the hour. He isn't seed any longer. He is vegetarian now, the lotus-vine in the pond, reaching to all the corners of my being.

Abba and Ammi have both gone out, leaving Ameena with me. She has lost some of her bluntness, or maybe she's being extra careful with me. I need care, they all think, and I don't want to disabuse them of any such notion, not till the baby comes, anyway.

I hear a car stop and the wrought-iron gate clang open. I know who it is. Ameena goes out to investigate. It is Jamal, she tells me, her face a little flushed.

'I know. Send him in.'

She is surprised at my lack of surprise. Such reactions always amuse me. Jamal looks just the same. Eight months don't always alter your physique. Ameena leaves us together. Jamal is civility itself, but he rambles, like a book slow to announce its theme. All the while his fingers play a tattoo on his kneecap.

'What brings you here, Jamal?'

'Must something bring me here? Can't I come just like that?'

'You can't. You are visiting your ex-wife, remember? Something must have brought you.'

I speak very gently, the way one does when teaching mathematics to a favourite but uncomprehending nephew.

'Ex-wife, eh? Ex!'

'Yes, Jamal.'

He again starts asking about my health and the baby's. We've been over all this already, I tell him.

'Whose is it?'

I laugh loudly, cruelly. I can't help watch the tension crawl over his face.

'Does paternity matter that much to you, Jamal?'

'Yes, damn it, it does. And you don't have to laugh your silly head off. You've no idea what a son means to...'

'A son? Whoever talked about a son? It could be a daughter. How would I know?'

'You didn't even tell me about the pregnancy! This...this is almost theft!'

I'm suddenly enjoying this. I'd like the suspense to last, like the long month I lived through after the first 'talaq.'

'Whose is it?' he has just asked. I can sense his tension. He is petrified of my answer.

'It could be the Passi's, you know.'

He does not absorb that too well. The eardrums take in the words, but don't translate them to the brain, perhaps. I nod, looking him in the eye, but with sympathy rather than defiance.

'It is the Passi's, I think,' I find myself telling his back, for he has already turned round to leave.

THE BRIDE RETURNS

(In memory of J.S. Sangha)

You drive better when you are angry. Gurpreet's eyes were focused far into the night, as far as the headlights of his black Mercedes could reach. He kept the speedometer needle leaning to the right of the 120-kilometre mark. On the Rudrapur-Moradabad road this could be a dangerous thing to do. The lime-washed trunks of shisham and mango trees flanking the road flashed by. Shadows and silhouettes scrambled for cover as the headlights roared past. The air was getting gradually thicker, little granules of mist coming up like an illusory wall, but disintegrating as the headlights came nearer. He preferred to drive with his lights dipped, not because of any concern for the oncoming traffic, but because he found that full lights got dissipated in the gathering mist.

Prabha spoke for the first time from the rear seat where she was sitting with Shivinder. 'You don't know when you come across a bullock cart on this road, or a stalled truck with iron bars sticking twenty feet out behind them, That wouldn't be nice.'

Yes, he thought, you don't mind carts coming towards you. The eyes of the bullocks flare like egg-size carbuncles in the headlights.

But if they are going in the same direction they could surprise one. The same went for the trucks, and a moving one was any day better than a stalled one. The speedometer needle did not waver one bit. The first time he slowed down was near the Rampur railway station where the roads from the Raza and the Buland sugar factories met the highway. And he had to slow down near the Kosi Bridge as also the Katghar Bridge over the Ramganga. The road bypasses had not come up by then.

Gurpreet's forehead was pimpled with sweat. A bad sign that. It showed the strain on him. The driver sitting alongside him with a shotgun in his lap must have noticed. But he was gazing impassively ahead. Gurpreet had kept his side glass down, yet the cold blast of early February air could not keep his brow from getting damp. Earlier he had been even more tense. Both Shivinder and Prabha had kept looking back apprehensively through the rear screen the moment the car touched the highway. 'Don't keep jumping around,' he had said irritably. 'No one's following us. And if someone does we will take care of him.' He had caressed the barrel of his shotgun, reclining in the lap of the driver.

You always wanted to be in the scrimmaging thick of it, Gurpreet, didn't you, you stupid bastard. Always felt yourself a cross between a Garibaldi and an Al Capone. Well now, you are in it, me lad, he said to himself.

It had all started so innocuously that evening with the snarling of his Bhotiya dogs. He wished they were with him now. They would have caught the colonel by his mangy scruff and done him in, true and proper. It was just five days back that they had emitted one of their deep-throated warning growls. A few moments later he heard the distant hum of the car as it lurched over the dirt track leading to his farm. Normally he saw the lights first but this car was obviously having trouble with its silencer. He had seen to it that the last two hundred yards of the track led straight to his L-shaped farmhouse. The fewer curves there were to a road the less chance there was of an ambush. And he had ensured that no hedges cluttered up the landscape. At least one acre of land had been wasted on a lawn around the house. Standing sugarcane (the only crop that he grew on his 200-acre farm in the Tarai) too near the house could spell danger. In a small dressing room which lay between the bedroom and the bathroom, he kept a loaded shotgun in the closet. Not that he had any specific enemy, but just in case. The 'culture' of the Rudrapur Tarai was such that one had to be on guard. To start with, his uncles had been hostile. This ragged boy who did not know how to tie his turban, who had wasted his time in college, he wanted his father's land back, did he? Over our dead bodies. He would let the whole farm run to seed as likely as not, and starve his poor mother! But Gurpreet had shown them his mettle. He had chucked college, returned and put up a shack—just a one-room affair of bamboo and straw—on his land. 'If you don't give me my 200 acres, I am going to set this entire cane crop on fire.' Oaths, threats, imprecations were exchanged. Finally they had given in. But these enmities were over and done with long since. Now it was his lifestyle which was attracting attention. He ran his farm so well he had put all the neighbouring farmers in the shade. During the summer an air conditioner hummed in his bedroom and another in the room where he kept his Bhotiya dogs. A huge refrigerator, which he had bought off an American Visiting Professor to the nearby Agricultural University at Pant Nagar, loomed in the dining room. He had opened a poultry farm and a dozen eggs rolled into two enormous omelettes would grace his breakfast table. All sorts of hangers-on crowded in, mostly for booze and some for the kick of it, the high life and the escapades. And then the turban was put away and he got his hair cut with almost as much nonchalance as if he was getting a hedge clipped.

The Bhotiya dogs he was thinking about had been snarling away. As the car negotiated the ruts, its lights acquired the lurching gait of a drunkard, now floundering into the dust of the road and now hitting the roof of the farmhouse, smack on its corrugated hide. The fellow should slow down, Gurpreet thought. The car hobbled through the last fifty yards as if trailing a broken limb.

As Gurpreet came out he found the man kneeling, taking a look at its underbelly. 'Hope you haven't broken your springs. I'm sorry it's a bad road. We haven't had it done up after the rains this time.'

The man stood up. 'Don't worry. Nothing's broken. The old lady will still run. And it's a lovely road. Better than some of the PWD things you have to drive on.' He laughed. This man wants something real bad, thought Gurpreet. The other man had wiped his right hand on his jeans and extended it.

'I'm Sparrow,' he said.

'Some sparrow,' said Gurpreet, eyeing the strapping figure of Shivinder, a good four inches taller than him. Both guffawed heartily.

'The name's Shivinder.'

'I'm Gurpreet. Call me Preet.'

'Billy Bakshi told me about you. I'm a great pal of his. Known each other since we were that big.' He gestured with his hand, touching his knee. 'If you ever go to Rudrapur, you must meet Preeti,' he had told me. 'So here I am.' Gurpreet managed a wry smile.

Shivinder had taken off his leather jacket and started stamping around in the verandah, shaking off the dust from his suede ankle-boots. He could hear the excited chatter of the servants, and saw from the corner of his eye one of the farm hands proceeding with a knife towards the poultry house. A quick bath and he had sat down with his host over a bottle of whisky. He studied Gurpreet carefully. There was no mistaking it—the man had an arresting physique. He could not be more than five feet and a half and yet he would be weighing the best part of three hundred pounds. But the fat and the flesh sat well on him. His wide, barrel chest and his thick neck took care of that. And he topped it all with a fleshy, bearded Hemingway face. It was not a forbidding face for it was slit with small kindly eyes. The only thing comical about him were his legs, short and slim, tapering to small, Chinese feet. On horseback the blighter would look impressive, thought Shivinder, provided of course the horse's spine did not cave in. Shivinder usually thought in terms of cowboy language for the simple reason that he had read little else. He was intrigued by the way the man downed his liquor. Gurpreet would fill half a tumbler with neat whisky, drink it in one gulp and a few minutes later wash it down with a pull at a soda bottle.

Where is the catch, thought Gurpreet. Being a friend of Billy Bakshi was fine, but what did Shivinder want? He did not have long to wait. As they drained the bottle, the story came out by bits. From the hints Shivinder had thrown about his lineage and his association with the royal house of a former princely state in Punjab, he sized Shivinder up for what he was, the drifting spawn of castaway royal sperm. Slowly, almost laconically, Shivinder came to the point. At Simla he had stuck up a friendship with Prabha, Colonel Dhillon's daughter. She was one of those girls always in the spotlight—debates, dramatics, elocution. 'The spouting whale gets harpooned,' said Gurpreet rather philosophically.

'You are right on the mark, man! I have just married her,' answered Shivinder.

'Married her?' asked Gurpreet incredulously. 'But she's just a kid.'

'What do you mean?' asked Shivinder rather defensively. 'She'll be nineteen in a fortnight.'

It had been a civil marriage. They had gone to the court, and that was that. Dhillon was a retired colonel who had a farm hardly a dozen kilometres from Gurpreet's place. A crusty old no-nonsense-man, Dhillon had believed in keeping his children with an iron collar round their necks. Somehow, he had got wind of his daughter's goings-on in Simla, had written to the Principal that he was withdrawing her from the college and had forbidden her to step out of the house.

'So the problem is how to spirit her away, is that it?'

'Well, that about sums it up, I suppose.'

'Kidnapping, in other words.'

'Come on now. I can't kidnap my own wife, dash it.'

'You never know. The law is a very funny bird,' concluded Gurpreet ruefully.

But there was very little that Gurpreet was not willing to do for a friend, or a friend's friend. Within a day he had commandeered vehicles. A farmhand dispatched to Colonel Dhillon's house returned with the information that in the evenings husband and wife often went out visiting, leaving the daughter under the care of an ageing Gurkha chowkidar. The next day Shivinder had managed to meet Prabha clandestinely in the evening and the escape plans were discussed.

Within five days the 'operation' was almost through. The next day Prabha had just to step across to the road at six in the evening and start walking towards the town. An Ambassador car with Shivinder and Gurpreet in it was to come from the rear, dip its lights twice, slow down and pick her up. It would be that simple! Two other cars were to follow them, each with two armed men. It was going to be a rumbustious affair and to hell with the law book.

But things did not work out to plan. The evening before the planned getaway Shivinder went to have his third clandestine meeting with Prabha. The Gurkha chowkidar spotted them and there was trouble. He was going to tell the Colonel. They pleaded. Prabha even touched his feet. But the man was adamant. He shook his head vigorously and started talking about loyalty and whose salt he was eating, that is, the kind of things that would have qualified him to become a scriptwriter for a Bombay movie. Eventually Shivinder got fed up. He smacked the Gurkha hard, put Prabha in his car and drove off. But the Gurkha was made of sterner stuff. He clung to the rear fender of the car. 'Let go or you will die. *Mar jaega,* shouted Shivinder, too afraid to put the car into fourth gear. For a hundred yards the chowkidar hung on desperately, right up to the main market square where he finally let go, bruised and battered, shouting away, '*Bhag gai*.' The Punjabi truck drivers' mechanics and others sitting at the dhabas and the tea stalls took up the chant, shouting, '*Pajh gai, Pajh gai*.' A town crier could not have made a better job of it. Years later, Gurpreet could never forgive the Colonel for slapping the Gurkha and sacking him.

Gurpreet, who liked to think of himself as a generalissimo, was a bit taken aback at all his plans being upset. Two borrowed cars were standing at the farmhouse, but the drivers had gone. The guns were there but the two hoods who were supposed to wield them were absent. One had to be prepared for a bit of blood spillage after all! There was nothing to be done now but to run for it. He packed all of them in his Mercedes, took some hard cash and a change of clothes and started off.

The bullock carts were still troubling him. Why couldn't they travel in daylight? Why couldn't there be a separate track for these blasted oxen? Why couldn't... He slowed down for the octroi barrier at Ghaziabad. A glance at his watch told him that he had made it in three hours flat. A half hour later he reached Delhi and checked into the Lodhi Hotel.

Despite a pot of black coffee, Gurpreet found himself stiff with tension two hours later and put through a call to Balbir Singh, a friend at Rudrapur. He heard a shrill-voiced telephone operator ask Balbir, 'Is that three zero five?'

'Yes.'

'Mr Balbir Singh'?

'Yes.'

'Call for you, sir!'

Gurpreet could hear Balbir shouting 'From where?' 'From where?' But the shrill-voiced lady probably had a cup of tea waiting and she just put Gurpreet through. 'Hello Chaudhry,' he said softly into the phone. Balbir was a Jat from Aligarh. He was well into his fifties now, a good fifteen years older than Gurpreet and the youngster's biggest hanger-on.

'Who's that? Who's that? Where the hell are you speaking from?'

'Kichha,' said Gurpreet and laughed throatily.

'Are you mad? Get out of there! Get out!' Balbir's voice sounded an octave shriller than the operator's. Gurpreet started feeling uneasy.

'Have they found out about me?'

'How naive can you get, Preet! Are you out of your damned mind? That fellow's car is still standing at your farm for all the world to see. You could've at least put it in a garage! What happened to you?'

Gurpreet was in no mood to answer his chief parasite. 'Have they gone to the police yet?' he asked.

'No, but they have hired Kakoo. You watch out.' Kakoo was a notorious hoodlum. Since he was certain that Gurpreet was not speaking from anywhere within fifty miles of Rudrapur, he let it be known that he had got a call from Kichha.

The same evening two jeeps bristling with guns had scoured Kichha, looking for Gurpreet.

The next few days they shifted from Lodhi Hotel to the Janpath and then to the Imperial. The reports from Rudrapur were getting more alarming. They would murder him in Delhi if they got the chance! He did not believe it. But then a friend from the Escorts Farm told him that an ugly-looking character was enquiring about Gurpreet at their Guest House in Delhi. That was ugly news. Eventually they flew to Calcutta. Another fifteen days there and things may cool off, they thought.

Sitting in the hotel lobby one day he asked Shivinder, 'You are married, aren't you? No doubting that I hope.'

'Of course we are! Proper civil marriage and all the rest.'

'Let's see the papers.'

He was appalled when he saw it. It was not a marriage certificate. It was a notice given by the court calling for objections to the proposed marriage. He could now be hit with half the law book, he reasoned. 'What's your age?' he asked Prabha.

'Nineteen.'

'But you did your Senior Cambridge only last year, didn't you? That would be a bit late.'

'I was a bit late as you call it, but Dad has it all fixed. Actually, I had to stay home one year because of typhoid. So when I changed schools Dad showed my age a year less.'

'So how old are you according to your school certificate?' he asked holding back a surge of apprehension.

'Why, I'll be eighteen on the twenty-sixth of this month, that's in another week's time,' she answered smiling.

'You'll be eighteen and I'll be damned,' he said, for once losing his patience. 'Before you're eighteen we will be in jail, don't you understand?' Good grief! She was a minor! That meant abduction, illegal confinement, rape, the works, marriage or no marriage, he thought.

In Calcutta he felt lonelier. He did not want to intrude on the couple, who at times seemed to him callously indifferent to what they had triggered off. Normally the city would have aroused his curiosity but now there was just the taste of bile on the tongue. He was now conscious of a slow, smouldering anger within him. Like cancer, his rage had a long latency period. Why did he *have* to get into this, he kept asking himself. Where do *I* fit in? How long do I have to chaperone these honeymooners who have not married? For two days he noticed around him a penumbra of anger, a sort of electrical field which one intruded into at one's risk. He shook his head vigorously when he realised this. He had to detoxify the atmosphere around him, get the demon out of his insides.

They returned to Delhi by train and checked into the Lodhi Hotel once more. They had been on the run for over three weeks by now.

'Isn't it your birthday day after tomorrow?' he asked Prabha.

'Yes.'

'Would you seriously mind if I were to tell you how to celebrate it?'

'No,' she answered.

'Get married.'

He called a Sikh priest, asked a few people over in Delhi and made Prabha and Shivinder go through the ceremony. What is more important, a photographer took about fifty snaps of the wedding, including the obeisance to the Granth Sahib and the seven circumambulations. As the Granthi and his assistant took up the chant, the nasally-intoned verses seemed to calm the troubled waters of his soul. For the first time in a month he felt at peace with himself and the world.

Two days later, armed with the photographs, they started back. The dust was settling, his friends at Rudrapur had told him over the phone. Yet at the Katghar Bridge on the Ramganga he had stopped. 'Something tells me things are not all right.'

'Come on, man, we will see what they can do,' said Shivinder with a put-on display of bravado. But Gurpreet shook his head. For hours they waited this side of the bridge making cautious enquiries if there were any ruffians at the other end waiting for them. Anyone with guns? Sardars? Peasant types? They could be in a jeep or two? No jeeps either. Still, Gurpreet had stalled, even at the risk of being considered yellow by Shivinder.

☛

Kaka Singh, alias Kakoo, was a resident of Dholewali Bhaini in Fazilka, a village on the Indo-Pakistan border. He had had his share in the use of the lathi and the spear—a riot here, a vendetta-murder there. Then he had quietly slipped off into the Tarai where many of his Rai Sikh kinsmen had lands. Here he had attained a certain notoriety by needlessly spearing to death a young amateur photographer who was trying to photograph the dead body of a man murdered by Kaka's friends. It was a mindless act which did his friends no good. While acquitting him, the Sessions Judge had passed strictures against the police. 'Where was the occasion for the accused Kaka Singh to have murdered the deceased? The prosecution has not bothered to prove any enmity between the two. I regret to say that I am not a believer in motiveless malignity. The prosecution has failed miserably...' etc. Since then Kakoo had been in great demand. He now sat in a truck parked on the Rampur end of the Katghar Bridge.

'Oi Mukha,' he said, '*Curnail di mat mari gai a*, the Colonel is off his nut. Why should the boy come back to Rudrapur? He will go to Bombay, Madras. Gurpreet will return. Where can he go? *Onoo apan vekh lavange*, we will take care of him when he comes.'

Mukhtar Ahmed, alias Mukha, was a resident of a border village in Pakistan fairly close to where Kakoo had lived. He had once traded half a tola of gold with Ghulam Hassan for a cow. Hassan pocketed the gold but forgot all about the cow. He was last seen returning to his village one evening, cycling along the canal bank. A month later, a skeleton was discovered in a field flanking the canal. Shortly afterwards, Mukha had crossed over, contacted his smuggler friends and followed Kakoo right up to Rudrapur. He now scanned the road with his basset-hound eyes. 'Twenty-four hours we have been sitting here like fools,' said Mukha. 'The Colonel is mad, I agree.' They were afraid of attracting the attention of the police, herded their cronies into the truck, and drove off.

☛

The next day Gurpreet and party drove into Rudrapur safely. It fell to Gurpreet's lot to beard the old lion, still licking his wounds. He left his Mercedes, took a jeep, put two of his flunkies behind and drove into the Colonel's house. Colonel Dhillon had been rehearsing this moment for a month, soliloquising to himself what exactly he would say to the daughter and the lover. And when he fantasised about Gurpreet it had been one long orgy in sadism. But when he found Gurpreet in front of him in actual flesh and blood, tweed and corduroy, the fleshy face with the beard, the pouched belly all atop the legs of a belly-dancer, all his fine phrases deserted him. His expression a study in misanthropy, all he could do was slap Gurpreet hard on his face. Gurpreet took it calmly, in deference to the old man's age and ire. But he saw through the bogus Sandhurst accent and the pathetic attempt to keep a stiff upper lip when he was plainly cracking under the emotional strain of the moment. Their conversation was short and to the point. Gurpreet told him clearly that the girl was legally married, that he was armed with proof and was ready to face any law court or panchayat.

Gurpreet pressed home the same point when he went to meet his own irate grandfather. Everything was above board. A proper, legal wedding that's what it was, and what's more, he could prove it! If the Colonel claimed that the girl was kidnapped, let him go to the police!

Eventually, a panchayat assembled—Gyanis, greybeards, farmers, even a retired General. The moment the photographs were produced, with Prabha beaming away, the whole balloon was pricked. Gurpreet now threw the gauntlet. 'Shall I call Prabha here to testify before everyone?' he asked. Dhillon did not rise to the bait. He just clasped his head in his hands in a tragic gesture of defeat, a battered hulk brought to his derelict knees. Gurpreet felt sorry for having done this. At least this final sword-thrust could have been delivered by Shivinder, he thought. Why did he have to make me do this?

The next day the entire Tarai was agog with the wildest rumours about the affair. They started saying that she used to meet Shivinder in the sugarcane fields when, of all things, she went there to do her morning business! As if the Colonel did not have a toilet in his house!

Shivinder and Prabha left. On reaching Punjab, Shivinder wrote a long, maudlin letter of thanks. Could he in some way recompense Gurpreet? 'After all, look at the cash alone you have spent on us.' Gurpreet wrote back saying that if they must, they could pay him for the air tickets for Calcutta which he had purchased for them. He received a cheque a month later for six hundred rupees from Shivinder. It bounced. He wrote back telling him about the fate of the cheque. Shivinder apologised profusely, and sent another cheque for six hundred. It bounced again. Gurpreet never wrote to him thereafter.

AND ON YOU ALSO BE PEACE

Mirza Koocha was the kind of place where people replaced the wrought-iron grilles of their balconies with material made out of packing cases, where the cotton carder's bow twanged in the morning as people brought out their old quilts and mattresses and got them redone; where a hawker of gram and puffed rice made good business as he handed out his paper cones; where boys played seven-tiles on the main square. It was the kind of place where a retired schoolmaster passed all his mornings in a neighbour's verandah reading newspapers. It had a small mosque with a cusp-shaped, horseshoe entrance, and a minaret you could touch if you took a high enough leap. Where the plaster had peeled off from the buildings you could still see nineteenth-century brickwork, thin brick held together with lime. At the foot of the only peepal tree in the area stood an ochre-coloured slab with Hanuman's image carved on it, the right hand holding aloft a mace and the left carrying a mountain. There was a wrestling pit, where at dawn you could hear grunts as people did their push-ups and swung their clubs to build up their shoulder blades and biceps. Mirza Koocha was an elegant adjunct to a grubby old city in 1880. It was now a seedy-looking adjunct to a garishly noisy city in the nineteen-eighties.

Stirring in her sleep Shalini had heard the reply to the salutation, not the first bit but the answer, clear as a bell, '*Waalaikum as-salaam*.' It must be the maulvi, she thought, in his tattered knee-length sepia-coloured coat, going to the mosque for the morning prayer. But she never heard the call to the faithful, the mind drugged with sleep having suddenly closed its antennae. She had missed the azan, rising like a plume of mist, a visible benign spirit disappearing into the skies.

But when she woke up, the sound and the sensation of the word stayed close to her like the memory of a happy dream: *waalaikum as-salaam*—what a treasure of sibilances and sonorities the Arabic salutation harboured: And on you also be peace.

She was still drowsy when the sadhu woke her up, banging on the door. He was black-bearded and big-bellied. A flowing saffron robe lent him considerable dignity, which neither his wits nor his learning entitled him to. Three horizontal bars of sandal paste traversed his wide forehead from temple to temple. He held a small brass bucket in his hand, while his disciple intoned slokas in Sanskrit which he punctuated with a clanging noise from a long pair of fire tongs he carried with him. Shalini felt a little peeved being shaken from sleep like this. Charity was all very fine and a few coins and a plateful of flour would not impoverish her; but it was disagreeable being dragged out of bed. '*Namo Narayan*,' cried the sadhu by way of salutation.

'*Waalaikum as-salaam*,' she replied mechanically, dropping a fifty-paisa coin in the brass bucket with a tinkle. But as she advanced to overturn a modest pile of flour into a bag carried by the disciple of the sadhu, she found him withdrawing it hurriedly. Both the sadhu and the neophyte disappeared, looking over their shoulders at her repeatedly, bewilderment on their faces. They hadn't even bothered to bless her, a normal custom when one gave alms. Shalini shrugged and went into the kitchen where she poured the flour back into a big tin box. She put tea leaves, milk, sugar and water in a kettle and lit the gas stove. Arranging two tumblers and a teapot on a tray, she waited for the brew to come to a boil. Pouring the tea through a strainer into the pot, she carried the tray to the bedroom, where she woke up her husband, Dev, and handed him a steaming tumbler. She wrapped a part of the pallu of her crumpled saree round the tumbler and started sipping the tea.

'Why did the fellow have to come so early?' asked Dev, his eyes still sticky with sleep.

'I suppose if you want your breakfast you start collecting it early. Otherwise only lunch, no breakfast, which would be rather sad.'

Through the veranda door a blade of light stole in and caressed her feet. Their neighbour upstairs started beating his rug. She could picture him holding a small, rectangular Shahjahanpur rug over the balcony and beating it with a stick. The dust came powdering down filtering into the room as quietly as the blade of light. Six trucks speeding past her house would not have raised so much dust, she thought.

She had a quiet hour sipping tea, reading the paper and indulging in amiable chatter. As she cleared the tray, she saw Bhatnagar, the retired schoolmaster who lived across the street, advancing towards their house. 'Not today! Not on a Sunday morning!' she exclaimed, exasperated.

'Well, I suppose, he wants his *news* early,' quipped Dev. That was the trouble with caste. If you belonged to the same community you could go and park yourself in your neighbour's bedroom. Bhatnagar came at about ten in the morning on weekdays, ensconced himself on a reed chair in the verandah and read the paper from cover to cover. Shalini did not mind because, while she finished her cooking and her laundry, he kept an eye on her two-year-old son, Vikram.

Shalini walked on to the verandah and waited for Bhatnagar, the look on her face as affable as dry ice. The schoolmaster called out, '*Namaskar*', without bothering to fold his hands in front of him for, after all, whoever folded his hands to someone thirty-five years younger? Impassively she answered, '*Waalaikum as-salaam*.' He reached out for the paper automatically, opened it and then felt the impact of her words.

'I beg your pardon?' he said, peering over the upper rim of his spectacles.

'*Waalaikum as-salaam*.'

The paper slipped through his hands and he gazed stupefied at the bindi on her forehead and yesterday's sindoor in the parting of her hair. Then, to Shalini's intense amusement, he retreated, looking over his shoulder even as the sadhu had done.

'How did you get rid of him that fast?' asked Dev, when she went in.

'I've got hold of a talisman, the key to all rebuffs.'

How does the grapevine work in a suburb, or anywhere else? How does gossip carry? It calls for research, the logistics of it. But something was afoot already, a vague unease, words exchanged in undertones, the raising of eyebrows and shaking of heads.

She finished her laundry, and gave a wash to Vikram while Dev languidly finished the paper. Even as Dev went off to bathe she found three people dismounting from their bicycles. By the time she went into the verandah they were already squatting on the reed chairs.

'Daughter, we are from the Sarvdeshik Hindi Parishad. We would like to talk to your husband,' said a stocky fellow in a shirt and dhoti, who was trying ineffectively to tuck his right heel under his buttocks as he sat cross-legged on the reed chair. 'My name is Misra,' he added as an afterthought. From his accent he appeared to be a Punjabi. She took a look at the others and liked them even less. One of them had a plume of hair tied into a knot at the rear of his cranium. Shalini did not relish being daughtered by anyone, least of all by people with crew cuts and knotted hair plumes.

'What business do you have with him?'

'That is no concern of yours, daughter. That is our concern,' said Mr Misra, smiling benignly. 'Meanwhile, could we please have a glass of cold water?' As she went in, Misra said to the others in a lowered voice, 'We must drink the water served by her. In fact, that is why I asked for it, to show that we harbour no prejudice.' The others nodded their heads as Shalini, her head covered with the pallu of her saree, served them water.

'Daughter, send your husband out.'

'One can send someone out if he is in.'

'You mean to say he is out?'

'If one is not in, he cannot help being out.'

'Where has he gone?'

'He went to Ferozabad today.'

'By train or by bus?'

'By bus. And he went to the bus stand by rickshaw.' She had already noticed the three exchanging glances, which seemed to say, 'What else did you expect with a wife like that? Can you blame the husband for running away?' She also noticed the schoolmaster, Bhatnagar, standing on the road and watching them carefully. The moment Bhatnagar found that he had been spotted he ducked for cover and disappeared from view. She found her anger rising. A strange neighbourhood this! Had she known of the kind of people she would have to live with, she would not have married! As the three gentlemen from the Sarvdeshik Hindi Parishad rose to leave, they said, 'Namaste.'

'*Waalaikum as-salaam*,' she answered, not wishing to see their faces ever again. '*Chee-chee*,' said the man with a crew cut, while those with the hair plumes nodded. Their worst suspicions seemed to have been confirmed.

'What is so *chee-chee* about it?' she asked.

'Well, one should stick to one's dharam,' said Misra.

She got agitated now. Who was he to lecture her about dharma and *adharma*, especially when he had the temerity to pronounce it as *dharam*? There isn't a word in Hindi which the Punjabi cannot murder while pronouncing it, she thought.

'And what is wrong with *waalaikum as-salaam*? All it means is "on you also be peace." What do you want people to wish you? Street fights?'

Well, well, she thought, as they looked exasperatedly at her and left, enough visitors for the day! Ever since she had married and come to Mirza Koocha three years ago, she had become accustomed to a dozen people dropping in on a holiday, someone to listen to the radio news, another to make a telephone call and leaving a fifty-paisa coin behind, despite protestations. But this morning had been exceptionally taxing. She had not even had the time to have a bath. She ran into the bathroom.

By now the news had spread. She had done it. She and that husband of hers, most probably, but he at least was ashamed of it, as one should be! Changing one's faith was not as casual a matter as walking across a street, after all. Or perhaps he had grown chicken-hearted, afraid of ancestral curses, or the end result of karma. No one liked being pushed fifty odd rungs down the transmigration ladder. Imagine another fifty births in a worsening India, a more crowded and a hungrier India, a dirtier India where more people spat and urinated on the streets and jostled with each other in the traffic than ever before! Imagine another fifty births among sycophants and crooks.

Anjanibir, a lecturer in the celebrated St. Xavier's College, heard it all with becoming gravity. His colleague Trinath Prasad was getting excited. So was that uncle of his, a certain Misra from the Sarvdeshik Hindi Parishad.

'Yes, the man is shamefaced,' Misra was saying, 'but the woman is more brazen about it. The *churail* was announcing it from the house-tops!'

'I'm telling you, Anjanibir Singh,' said Trinath, 'Meenakshipuram is here, just as 1984 is here and now, and so is *Asht-grah*, if you ask me, the eagle and the bear locked in combat.'

'We will keep Nostradamus out of it if you don't mind,' said Anjanibir, annoyed. He knew his colleague was addicted to astrology. 'Are you sure this couple you talk about has been converted?'

'I'm not hundred per cent sure. I'm two hundred per cent sure,' said Misra.

'We can't take everything lying down and let events roll over us, and just sit around twiddling our thumbs.' Even as he said this Anjanibir realised he was being facetious.

'The choice,' said Misra, 'is between doing something and not doing something.'

As the Secretary of the Virat Arya Pratinidhi Sammelan, Anjanibir was not in favour of getting involved in individual cases. This did not accord with his perceptions of his own role. He was there to plan social reform. He was not a concierge to resist gate crashing proselytes. 'What exactly do you want me to do?' he asked, irritated.

'Let's go and talk to the husband. Let's admit that the system has been harsh on certain castes. But that does not mean that they have to leave...'

'All right,' interrupted Anjanibir, 'let's go.'

And that is how, when Shalini came out crisp and fresh from her bath and stood before the mirror to fill the parting in her hair with sindoor and apply the circular bindi on her forehead, she was dismayed by the murmur of voices coming from the drawing room. Who could it be now? People just crawled all over you in this place. Was this a house or a market square? It was past noon now and turning just a little warm. She walked into the crowded room to check on how many people might need to be served a cold drink or so.

There were five visitors in the room, but her attention was soon riveted to just two of them. One was a burly man with a moustache, whom the others referred to as Trinath Ji. The other was called Professor Sahib. Trinath was railing against the system. 'The humiliations and the discriminations against your brethren have been enormous, sir. We hang our heads in shame.' What discrimination was he talking about, she wondered. Anjanibir, lean, olive-coloured and handsome, whom the others referred to as Professor Sahib, now spoke up.

'Where the hungry are concerned, each one with a full belly has to feel contrite. Similarly, when we talk of deprivation every one of us has to feel guilty.'

Shalini nodded. The man was talking sense. Trinath took the cue.

'The clean have to feel guilty for the dirty work which a chosen few have to perform. We have to feel for those who live in slime, below the poverty line.'

The man spoke in internal rhyme she thought. A minute later he said, 'There is no paucity of atrocities on you.'

Quickly, she groped for something to throw back at the burly Trinath. Phrases flashed across her mind. 'No lack of back.' No, that was not good enough. Then it came.

'No dearth of girth,' she said involuntarily, startling everyone. 'I'm sorry,' she said, not daring to look at her husband, who stared at her in disbelief. She hastily went out and brought in some orange squash, as if in atonement. She found Dev still staring at her icily. Concentrating on the conversation, she found random phrases sticking to her: 'lip sympathy', 'faith-switch', 'scapegoats', 'the violated and the vulnerable', 'emancipation.' When Anjanibir spoke, she found the phrases a little more difficult to grasp, 'crystallisation of unrest', 'society, horizontally stratified', 'mainstream of Hinduism' and the like. Once Trinath turned to her and said dramatically. 'You are the children of God.'

'I am the daughter of Kedar Nath,' she answered. And a little later, when someone suggested that there was no earthly reason why she should not be allowed to draw water from a well, Shalini was incredulous. 'Well! We get water from the tap. Don't you see that storage tank overhead? Imagine me walking to a well with a pitcher on my head!' The little room rang with peals of her laughter. Even Trinath was abashed for a moment.

What were they talking about? she kept wondering. There had to be a forum for this kind of discussion. You can't just drop in on strangers and start off on social reform or capital punishment or euthanasia! She spoke out, as always, without thinking, involuntarily almost.

'If you really have the Harijans on your minds, it won't do you any good to just talk about them sitting on your arses.' Had a shell or meteor landed in the room the visitors could not have been more stunned. Their mouths fell open like trapdoors, their pupils dilated, their eyebrows were jacked up. Trinath was the first to muster his dignity as he fiddled a little nervously with the gathers of his crumpled dhoti.

'We are *not* sitting on our arses,' he said ponderously.

'Then what are you sitting on?' she asked. Before he could answer, Dev pounced upon her, 'You have absolutely no sense... no idea of what you say. The first thing that comes into your mind you blurt out.'

'I'm just telling them to go out in the open, in the bastis, the slums, the Harijan colonies. It's no good sitting here and talking of the emancipation of Harijans. They have come to the wrong place.'

'We have come to the *right* place,' said Trinath vehemently. 'If we cannot talk of social reform in the house of a...a member of the weaker section, where else can we discuss it?' Trinath was struggling to control his indignation. His upper lip quivered with suppressed resentment.

'Weaker section?' It was Dev's turn now to fly off the handle. 'Who the hell do you think you are? Who the hell do you think *we* are? We are descended from Todarmal himself—yes, Raja Todarmal of Akbar fame. We are among the highest Kayastha families in town.' He trotted out his genealogy, showed them the fibrous roots of his family tree and then showed them the door. As they stepped out of the verandah, considerably chastened, they saw four men led by a short frail old man with a trimmed salt-and-pepper beard, dressed in a sherwani. He wore a white muslin skull cap. All of them were wearing sherwanis, all of them had caps, all of them had beards. Shalini recognised the maulvi from his sepia-coloured coat. This was the last straw for the members of the Virat Arya Pratinidhi Sammelan. Those fellows in sherwanis had come to collect the spoils, they thought. 'Congratulations,' said Trinath bitterly. '*Tasleem*,' said a man with a henna-coloured beard, who bowed rather low, and gave Trinath an exaggerated salaam.

The man with the henna beard, which had the colour of a maple leaf in autumn, was called Karim Mian. He now advanced and threw his arms around an astonished Dev in a bear-hug. The others repeated the performance, each shouting, '*Mubarak ho*, Dev Mian, *mubarak ho*!' Dev hadn't the foggiest idea of what the felicitations were about, and he was really hungry now. This endless stream of visitors had denied him his lunch.

'It's a very bold step, Dev Mian, a very bold step', said the frail old man whom the others referred to as Anees Bhai. He's probably referring to my having booted out Trinath and co., thought Dev. '*Der aae per durust aae*, you came late, but you came correctly,' said Anees Bhai wagging his head.

Then there was a slightly embarrassing silence. Anees Bhai cleared his throat and continued, 'All things happen by God's immutable decree, except evil and injustice, which can never be attributed to God, but to man.' Dev tried to take in all the theological intricacies in that one short statement. But he refrained from commenting, because that could involve him in an argument, and each argument would mean lunch postponed by another twenty minutes.

'To what do I owe the pleasure of your coming here?' asked Dev, finally.

'To the pleasure of *your* coming,' answered Karim Mian, as they all burst into laughter.

'This is getting to be a bit esoteric, isn't it?' asked Shalini, as ever, without thinking. 'One doesn't know who has come to whom.'

'Does the dream come to the night, or does night come to the dream?' asked Karim Mian, looking around for applause. Shalini could not help mimicking him. 'Does sleep come to the eyelid or does the eyelid go to sleep?' She hoped the sarcasm had gone over their heads. She yawned and went off to get some cold water for the visitors. Dev excused himself for a minute and followed her.

'This is getting to be much too much,' hissed Shalini. 'Who the hell are they?'

'I don't know, for the life of me.' He noticed that Shalini was near to tears.

'But why us?' she asked, distraught. 'Why must they all descend on us and, of all days, today?'

'Yes, yes,' said Dev. 'Now all I've come to say is, don't say something silly. I don't want another scene.'

Shalini had had enough of this. 'Who's talking? It was you who booted them out and I have no regrets. If people choose to mistake us for sweepers, they deserve to be swept out.'

'All right, all right,' Dev tried pacifying her and went back to the crowded room. Meanwhile there were hurried confabulations in the room in Dev's absence. Anees Bhai had been the first to lean forward and warn the others in a half-whisper, 'Let no mention be made of the burqa.'

'Nor of circumcision,' added Karim Mian.

'But she's still putting sindoor in her hair,' expostulated the maulvi. 'That will have to go.'

'As also the bindi,' remarked Karim Mian. Anees Bhai inhaled deeply, more in despair than anger. 'Don't rush them. They are new to the fold,' he counselled.

Shalini brought in the cold water along with two small bowls containing sweet paan and some aniseed. Since Karim Mian was sitting nearest the door she offered the bowls to him first. Karim indicated the maulvi, who in turn passed her on to Anees Bhai as the senior-most in the party. Anees Bhai came up with a sham protest. 'Among us all are equals.'

'We will start with the first among equals,' said Dev out of politeness.

Anees Bhai took his glass of water and a pinch of aniseed, which he started chewing.

'No,' he said, 'we have no first among equals in our society. High and low, all are equal. Everyone eats at the same table. Khan and peasant, all are equal.'

'Except the women, isn't it?' blurted out Shalini. 'They must cover their faces and share a husband.'

This young woman was too sharp-tongued for Anees Bhai's liking, but he let it pass. Vikram, their two-year-old son, ambled in.

'What's his name?' asked Anees Bhai benignly.

'Vikram.'

'O, Viqar, Viqar Husain.' He turned to the others for approval. They all nodded their heads.

Shalini didn't like that. Her father's boss, an Englishman, had always addressed him as Sylvester, rather than Srivastava. For the rest of the family it had been a big joke. But even as a child Shalini had found it intolerable. Why can't he call you by your name, she had always fumed. If they mentioned 'Viqar' again she would put them where they belonged. For the present she held herself in check, smiled innocently and said, 'When I have a daughter I am going to call her Lakshmi.'

'Laeeq,' corrected Anees Bhai, looking to the others, who, like obedient marionettes again nodded their heads. It was bad enough, they thought, that Dev and Shalini were not changing their own names. But this woman was even consigning her future progeny to the Hindu pantheon. What kind of a conversion was this? Karim Mian had had enough.

'She's going to be Lakshmi and nothing but Lakshmi,' said Shalini, gritting her teeth.

'That she can't be,' said Karim Mian, shaking his head. 'And while we're about it, that bindi will have to go.'

'Where?' she asked, baffled.

'Well I don't know about that, but it will have to move out from your forehead. And so will the sindoor.'

'What about the sindoor?' she asked, incredulous. This couldn't really be happening, not in her own house.

'Well, that too will have to move out,' said Karim Mian firmly.

'Before that happens, Mr Cheeky Mian, you will have to move out from here! Now!'

There was a right-royal row. Voices turned shrill like the high-decibel clatter of cutlery. A small crowd had collected outside, Bhatnagar among them, as Karim Mian and company left in a huff. The telephone rang. Angrily Shalini picked it up.

'Is that 37472?' asked a tentative voice.

'Yes.'

'This is the Niamatullah-Rehmatullah Gulf Employment Agency. *Salaam waalaikum*.'

'Namaste,' replied Shalini with all the asperity at her command.

There was a pause. The voice asked rather laboriously, 'Is that 37472?'

'Yes.'

'*Salaam waalaikum*.'

'Namaste,' she said vehemently again. The line went dead.

HIGH PASTURES

He sits there, still as an icicle, his head resting on his forepaws. His eye twitches open now and then, taking in the entire darkening valley that lies before him. Special care has been taken to make him feel snug. A small rug, no bigger than a prayer mat, has been thrown over a bed of tattered leaves, so that he can lie comfortably on it. Varun has sat with him for long spells, the dog snuggling up to him and resting his wounded snout on the boy's thighs. There are deep scratches above his right eye, but threads of caked blood have prevented the skull from showing. His flanks are scarred and now and then he whines, almost inaudibly.

He is shaggy and big and black, and so they call him Kalu. He is used to lying around the whole day, his eyes seemingly closed in sleep. Lowing cattle, keening kites, cawing jackdaws would fail to stir his eyelids. Yet he is known to spot a pilgrim a mile off, or anchorite or beggar. There is nothing so evanescent that he cannot latch on to, not a low cloud scudding over the valley, not a breath of mist suddenly storming the high pastures of Aali and Vedni where his flocks have always browsed. He would sniff the air as if to see whether the mist was friendly enough. That done, he would resume his somnolence.

Kalu's vigilance is a study in mystical states. It is uncanny how the slightest movement at the far edge of distance would alert him. His eye would open like the third eye of Shiva in a B-grade mythological movie. Before this injury, less than a day old, not a shadow could stir anywhere in the valley without eliciting a guttural growl from his surly throat. His gaze was as distant as the valley was long, as the pastures were far-spread, as the flanking hills were high. And yet he would lie there, still as a sniper on a hill. It was only in the evenings that he would be suddenly galvanised into a growling bundle of energy, circling the herd and sometimes positively charging as he drove the sheep into their pens.

He belongs to Devi Singh. Devi Singh's hands are always warm, for they are forever around a chillum, which in its turn has always had a fresh coal fire in it. He has smoked his life away, his lungs thickly patched with nicotine. The last four years have been especially bad, with the elder son just disappearing like valley mist. The youngest, Varun, who has just entered his teens, looks almost tearful, afraid that the dog will die.

A cousin has already traversed the valley looking for a vet or a doctor, someone who might have drifted into the valley to tinker with the myth or invent a theory about Rupkund and its frozen dead. He has gone down to Mundoli, and after a one-mile descent to Bakrigarh, crossed the Kali Ganga and that freak mountain torrent that can now and then misbehave, Bhanwar Gar. Perhaps he may have gone right to the foot of the valley to Dewal in search for the medic or compounder, anyone who can heal a brave dog who has been in the sweating, scrimmaging thick of the fight of his life. A dog who is still alive merely because of his spiked collar, a six-inch-wide piece of stinking leather studded with pointed brass spikes.

They live in Wan, a cluster of a dozen or so large-sized hamlets spread all over a mountain, thickly wooded with oak, ringal and rhododendron. And conifers in plenty. Beyond lies the bare ridge of Ranakdhar. A half day's march after crossing the Soleh Gadera and walking along a bridle track flanked with buckwheat and phappar brings one to the Aali Bugyal—mile on mile of downy high-altitude pastureland, running along the ridge, north to south, till about three miles or so later it runs into the higher and even bigger pasture known as Vedni Bugyal. That's where the beautiful stone temple of Mahisasur-Mardini stands. The Aali pasture is dotted with crude stone sheepfolds, and makeshift huts towards the leeward side of the ridge, for the shepherds to lie up. Four hundred yards or so beneath the ridge top stretch the fir forests, where once in a while panthers are supposed to lurk.

Throughout the summer it is just two dogs, Kalu and Moti, who look after the flock as it browses its way through Aali. Moti is not exactly as big as Kalu. He is brown, except that there is a black patch that runs along his snout and bisects his head, as if a gene has been split and a dark colour added hypodermically. And it is left to Varun to keep them company, for his elder brother Kunwar Singh had gone off—no one knows where.

☛

He had left when hoar frost had already made its appearance on the higher reaches. Scorched leaf littered the ground. In less than a week, they would have moved down from the high pastures. It rained that afternoon, a high altitude rain, thin and drizzly, like pine needles dropping in a high wind. The after-rain mist hung low over the pasture and flocks of cloud settled over sheep flocks, moistening their flanks.

Next morning Varun had found only his brother's blanket and guessed what had happened.

Kunwar was damned if he was going to stay among the same mountains for a lifetime. There had to be more to life than fleecing wool, and lying down in smelly huts reeking of sheep flank and sheep turd, and honest to God it was difficult to tell which smelt worse. Year after year he looked out for the Devi's procession, with the same bright veils adorning her statue, the same conch cries and the same pujari with the same flywhisk. Poverty and buckwheat, poverty and sheep flocks, poverty and firewood on the backs of the women; only the forests seemed to get further and further away, and the firewood harder to get by the year.

He didn't go by the beaten track through Mundoli and Bakrigarh, right down to Dewal. He took a circuitous way through the Haat Pithwar and the Oona pasture to the Baang village. He crossed the Kail Ganga, and came to the steep climb on to the Lohajung saddle. He couldn't afford to lie up anywhere, for the night was too cold, brilliantly clear and flaring with stars.

In less than a week he was at Karanprayag. He worked as a labourer for a while, carting loads on his back from the bus stand below, to the town on the upper slope. This seemed civilisation to him, the pilgrim route to Badrinath chockfull of bus convoys, anchorites walking up all the way from Haridwar and Rishikesh, tourists with transistors and cameras. And once he had enough money he boarded the bus to Badrinath. Not that people did not advise him against it. No one goes there when the temple is about to be closed. Inauspicious. He went up to Joshimath and then some fear kept him from going further. Better to come here in the summer, he decided.

Then he fell in with the Bhotiyas. They were migrating from Mana with yak and mule, their harness bells reminding him of the clankle-clonkle of his own sheep. They drank chang, their home-brewed barley, and they laughed and their women laughed with them. The faces of the men glowed red as if some driftwood fire was reflected in their cheekbones. And the faces of the women glowed like the pearls of Basra, white and smooth and glossy, unblemished to the last pore. As they moved camp day after day, he drifted with them down the valley till they reached Srinagar, from where they branched left towards Kotdwar, he along with them.

There was no place in the world, he thought, that these Bhotiyas had not been to. They had traversed the length and breadth of Hundesh, Tibet, before the war with the Chinese had broken out. They knew the foothills, and were equally at home with the elephant grass in the Tarai, and mountain and moraine on the lower fringes of Tibet. And they knew those inhospitable tracts of Lapthal and Sanchemalla, arid and cold and stony, from where oxygen itself ran away and where all you came across were fossil stones. Death itself could be fossilised in this kind of terrain.

And over a tumbler of chang they regaled him with their stories. Hadn't he heard about Lapthal and Kungri-Bingri? They wouldn't believe it. A child would know all that—a Marcha child. Hadn't he heard that a great, terrible bird of prey lived in the Gauri glacier, and ate up at least one hairy person in the valley every day? Incidentally, they were all hairy, right down to their tongues, the people who inhabited the valley in those days. Who would rid the valley of this pest—the predatory bird, not the hairy people? Who but a levitating lama who had been all over through Astral Flight

Airlines. The lama, through his magic, sent a servant with bow and arrow and guide to kill the bird of evil. As they crossed the pass, the guide changed himself to a dog, and hence the pass became known as Kungri-Bingri, after that. Disguise was necessary at every turn, hence he turned himself into a stag, and the place became known as Dol-Dunga. At the next pass the guide turned himself into a camel, and it became known as Unta-Dhura. And when he slept for a night in a cave, he became a tiger so that the bird did not attack him and the place became Dung-Udiyar. Lastly, to allay all suspicion, he turned himself into a hare, and the place was named Samgaon. And that is how the first route to Tibet got marked. And needless to say the bird was shot dead with the lama's arrow. But the guide refused to stay in this inhospitable tract on the plea that there was no salt. And the Lama sprinkled salt throughout the valley so that human beings could stay here.

Kunwar Singh's eyes popped out. He had never heard such stories, never met such people. They never bothered to ask about his caste, or family or gotra. They just took him in and considered him one of themselves. He had been told from his childhood days that they were shifty-eyed and devious and, of course, unclean. Their ways were not the ways of the Garhwali. Liquor and meat have always been passports to Mlechchahood, and the Bhotiyas partook of both, in ample measure.

☛

The wind whines around the grass hut. The door rattles but the sound is deadened by a padding of dry grass on the frame. Its hinges squeal, however. When Kunwar Singh enters he finds that his father takes quite a while to give any sign that he has recognised him. It's four years since he met him last and half the light seems to have gone out of the old man's eyes. Even his hearing seems impaired.

An uncomfortable silence at the end of which Kunwar, noticing the stammer of the door against the frame, refers to the wind. Devi Singh nods his head.

'I may be deaf, but the grass hut listens to the wind.'

After some tea and hot chapattis, the father's cataract-clouded eyes seem to ask Kunwar where exactly he has been all this time. It is difficult to compress four years into half a night. The answer has of necessity to be a mixture of staccato responses, evasions, large chunks of monologue and silences succeeding each other. Slowly Kunwar thaws and the river of his narrative starts running beneath the ice, perhaps just articulate enough to be heard. The sequence gets jumbled up and he talks of going into the Tarai with the Bhotiyas before he comes to the bit about slinking away from home. But when he does, he tells it the way it happened, the track he took, the bus he boarded, the blanket left behind (whys and wherefores), the places he worked at. It is only when he speaks of the Bhotiyas that he gets animated, and his face lights up with memories as if they were fireflies. The trip to the Tarai gets short shrift. But he dwells at length on the upward trek to Joshimath and Mana in spring, the floral largesse of a solitary almond tree against the winter-charred hills; a ledge still tartarred with ice, as it lies in perpetual shadow; stacks of juniper drying on the rooftops at Mana, even as chillies would dry and turn colour on roofs in Wan.

And the images keep flitting before his eyes—a tilak on the beam overarching the main doorway; a shaman, with his braids flailing away as his neck and torso rotate in a circular frenzy; a woman with a Tibetan head dress of silver; fistfuls of barley being thrown to the wind gods as they depart towards the higher pastures. He seems to be bringing the Bhotiya villages to life, notched ladders, shallow winnowing baskets, grain drying on the terrace, smoke hanging low, the prods resting against the wall, the firewood basket on the female back.

Where is all this leading to? There has to be a payment for all this, the old man mumbles to himself. You can't just walk off one fine morning as if your family does not exist, or is dead, and think that nothing will happen. The karma bill has to be settled.

'What happened to the woman?'

This, just when Kunwar's monologue has at last run dry and he is about to turn in. At the best of times an expression of any kind is hard to come by on his father's gnarled face. More so now, as Devi Singh takes a big pull at the chillum. The cataract makes his eyes impervious to any probing.

'What woman, Father?'

'At the end of all this there has to be a woman, isn't it?'

Kunwar doesn't answer. He turns on his side and fatigue takes over, and dreams of slow-motion yak caravans moving over regions desiccated with cold; the lashings getting tightened as salt bags are strapped to the sides; cries of 'Lhagyalo', 'may the gods be victorious' as they set out; 'hoaaah', 'hoaaah' someone urges the yaks on; scenes changing, a blaze of frost at first light, and then the slow fade-out, valleys seen through the filter of heat and haze, and sounds filtered through, and confused with, other sounds, like the high singing wind around the grass hut, for instance.

The wind dies down in the morning: frost dazzles for a while and melts, as Kunwar Singh sleeps on. Kalu slobbers behind the herd as it moves towards the pasture. A bitch strays in, rust in colour and long of snout, followed by two shaggy looking curs who snarl at each other. She is graceful and coy and trips along with mincing steps, and Kalu breaks from the herd and follows her. He is not heard of again till the evening when the panther emerges from the oak forest and charges, laying about him fretfully amidst a gale of scuffed fleece and tangled horns and a collective bleat from the herd rising in a crescendo.

Kalu returns even as the panther is dragging away a slaughtered ewe. It is then that the fight begins. Kalu and Moti attacking jointly, one from the front and the other going for the hind legs. Each time the panther goes for the neck, the large spiked collar saves the dogs, but Kalu bears the brunt of the feline's claw marks. What with the hollering from other shepherds, and the two desperate dogs, the panther slinks back into the oak forest.

The long search for the vet, the valley traversed with the same urgency as when he had abandoned it years ago. A turmeric poultice for claw-mark and wound. Wind testing the bamboo door of the grass hut, or an autumn later, the grass door of a bamboo hut. Does it really matter? And the flock moving back to Lohajung. 'Whoaa! Whoaa!' Dreams crowding in thick as night fog, thick as the sweat of a Bhotiya woman as she snuggles up to you under a blanket of goat hair; the texture of the dream thick, yet the landscapes of the dream empty, like a region scarred with the movement of black ice and all its erasures. And the weather clearing over the eyelids, dandruff and snow borne away and visions of the blue river emerging from the blue mountain, and the white river out of the turmeric forest. And when the door creaks open and light shambles in, the fog at sunrise is as thick as the fog that had blotted out the previous evening.

BIRD ISLAND

He wouldn't tell his host that it was in a way the tenth anniversary. All the fun would go out of the trip. His wife never forgot the day, and never refrained from reminding him the day her son had vanished.

His host, the nawab of Shamasabad, as fine a gentleman as ever there was, had prepared for this excursion with considerable care. He had got his guns oiled and cleaned with a rag. And he had stocked enough twelve bore cartridges to shoot each denizen of a game reserve, leave alone a duck shoot in the wetlands known as *khadir* here.

The guns, he noticed, were the best in the line, a James Purdey and two Holland-and-Hollands. The butt of one of the guns had inlay work on it and the other had a mother-of-pearl coat. When he held them he was amazed how light they were. The nawab was a bit embarrassed when asked if they were custom made. (For, in that case, the price would be sky high.) Yes they were, he said reluctantly, and then his ten-year-old nephew showed Sudhakar the one meant for deer and boar shoots and the one for birds.

He realised he was a novice. He had always thought that guns were the same, it was the cartridges, rather the pellets in the cartridges, which defined the target. Yes, tigers and leopards would need a different weapon, one could imagine, but the others?

Logistics were left to his friend's friend, Colonel Majumdar. Sudhakar was told that the colonel was meticulous about details. The boat would be his. Sudhakar was a bit reluctant to tell the nawab that he had of late lost the appetite for going after game, big or small.

'Where exactly are we headed tomorrow, nawab sahib?' Though they had been friends for ages, the mode of address was always formal from both sides. Of course, you couldn't address royalty by first name. And royalty itself was so polite, the manners so impeccable, that you almost felt out of sorts.

'Don't worry, we are boating along the Ramganga, downstream of course. We'll be up much before dawn since we have to drive at least thirty miles to the river. The road, as you saw this morning, isn't too good.'

Sudhakar didn't feel like riddling the taciturn, slightly rotund nawab with a salvo of questions. They had been to the same school, though the nawab had been there some years earlier. Still, it was a bond of sorts. He had retired from his job and the nawab had asked him to come.

Twenty years ago, the nawab and he had fished in the Gomti together. Earlier the nawab had come with a *baraat* and he had been asked by the bride's father to 'entertain' the nobleman. That's how they had got to know each other. The hills were his beat and Sudhakar had invited him later to fish for trout in the Pindar. And they had trekked together.

The nawab looked soft, but he could walk a good fifteen miles a day, and he didn't flinch or look tired in the evening.

Absence can be heavy; it can weigh you down. It had made Sudhakar's shoulders droop for over ten years now. His son had walked out on them and there was no way they could find him. 'Not the police,' his wife Hemlata had said. She was afraid of the courts and the black-robed ones, whether on the bench or the bar. Her father had been caught in a land dispute with his cousins, in cases and appeals that had gone on for years. Litigation under the law the British had left us with was a sort of a *chakravyuha*, a roll of barbed wire in which you got entangled for life. 'He could have come under a truck.' Sudhakar had suggested to his wife one day, and she had refused to speak to him for a week.

She had been visiting astrologers, believed in sadhus and holy mantras of not-so-holy men. A havan had been organised in the house, wood-fire and ghee and a tonsured pujari with a hoarse voice—and of course, white sheets spread on the floor. A red thread had been sanctified by prayer and then tied round his wrist. That much he had allowed on his wife's insistence. He had no time for pandit and pujari, had cultivated distaste for saffron and ochre, these supposedly spiritual signposts. But what can you do but humour your wife who has lost her son?

The son Sukhdeo had always been too quiet—speech had landed on the child's tongue after he had crossed the age of three. Did he have enough friends in college, his parents had kept wondering. He stayed in his room upstairs on the second floor—just his room and the wide windy terrace lined with flower pots. Of course, there was a TV antenna fixed there—even though TV and its Doordarshan avatar were new to the country. They had given him a small set but he never switched it on, or almost never. He had his tape deck though and played his Kishori Amonkars frequently.

Sudhakar avoided going up and prying.

Hemlata would egg him on. 'See what he's up to? Can't you do even that?'

Let him have his privacy, he would tell her.

'What privacy! What privacy from father and mother! He should be sitting with us and chatting or going out with friends. I wouldn't mind if he got drunk somewhere, and beat up someone, or got beaten up. Even a brawl would be better than this clo-cloi—what is the word?'

'Cloistered living, you wanted to say.'

She would nod. He had a knack of knowing what she wanted to say, rather where she got stuck.

He'd shake his head in disbelief. 'He is a brooder.'

'What is that supposed to mean?' she'd ask, agitated.

'He broods.'

'You say this so matter-of-factly, as if it was the naturelest thing in the world to brood! *Wah*!' Her grammar went awry when her temper rose.

He'd just shrug—the best gesture invented to date when faced with angry wives.

He had asked her one day—that was two years after their son disappeared—if what had happened to her father was the only reason why she resisted going to the 'authorities.'

Yes, it was, she had said.

But he had seen her eyes turn evasive and her lips quiver.

He had persisted.

She eventually came out with it. What if the police confirmed their worst fears? What if they dug out the bones of some buried jackal and said, These are your son's skeletal remains?

He had tried to allay her fears. She was being paranoid, he had told her, and then couldn't resist an aside—no one buries jackals.

She had lost her temper. 'You know damn well what I mean. I don't mean the police will hand me bones of a jackal or dog or hyena. Even I know that. Some beggar's bones, some unclaimed dead body lying in the mortuary ...'

He didn't say a thing, though he had felt like telling her they wouldn't do a thing like that.

She quietened down and then with considerable effort had said, 'Suppose Sukhdeo is dead and they confront me with that?'

He had no answer. When facts turn brutal, not many people want to face them.

She had hinted at irrefutable proof—clothes and things, the gold chain he always wore, the two strands of that sanctified red thread which were wound around his left wrist.

☛

They got into the nawab's two-coloured Chevrolet at first light. It was then that Sudhakar summoned up the courage to tell him that now his shooting was restricted to the camera shutter. He would not like to carry that Holland-and-Holland, honoured though he was. He had held it once and just the feel of it had sent a thrill through him. But a resolve was a resolve. For years, he hadn't touched a gun. If the nawab was disappointed or surprised at his friend's reaction, he didn't show it. He just smiled benevolently and let it go at that.

They drove to the Ramganga, the river which divided the districts of Farrukhabad and Shahjahanpur. On each bank he could see a swathe of sand, now and then pockmarked with patches of grass. The boat was there, and Colonel Majumdar who commanded the Rajputana Rifles, or Raj-Rifs in army slang. The boat was decked with a rug and a cushion to sit on; there were two rowers in army fatigues and a mess *aabdar* in turban and achkan to serve breakfast and then beer. His paraphernalia, which included a primus stove, was spread over one corner of the boat.

The colonel had thought of everything. There were even straw hats to shield his guests from the winter sun later in the day.

Colonel Majumdar, a genial moustachioed man, had his own gun. They started rowing upriver. The nawab introduced Majumdar as a fast bowler in his young days. Sudhakar, a keen cricketer himself, exchanged some stories with him. The colonel told them how he had got Pataudi caught in the slips in the first innings. But in the second, the man stood a yard out of the crease and smashed Majumdar all over the park.

The sun was up now and he saw a gull almost resting on the water and for a moment dreaded that the boat would go over and smother it. Sudhakar looked down and saw the gull's image plummeting into the river even as it rose. He wondered if he had got them on camera, both bird and image. He would develop the film in his darkroom. The sight, unforgettable as it was, forgotten for the moment. His thoughts focussed on whether the bird would be clear and sharp and its image in the water aqueous, almost mystical. He started wondering if all that was mystic wasn't slightly smudged, and if haze and the mystical could be said to be of the same ilk. He was woken up from his reverie when he heard the sound of laughter; the colonel and the nawab were in splits.

'Where were you?' asked the colonel.

'In my darkroom,' he answered. He proceeded to educate them about his darkroom, his sophisticated camera, the wide-angle lens and why he developed his own films.

They passed lowing cattle, cowherds clicking their tongues as they moved to the grazing grounds. A bird went up and he thought of a receding ellipse.

Breakfast time: The *aabdar* had tea ready by now and was serving it along with sandwiches. The nawab murmured that the birds would hear the clatter of fork and plate, cup and saucer. Sudhakar saw a few birds flying away, but thought nothing of it, his mind occupied with omelette and toast and the tea he was drinking.

Breakfast over, the two shikaris with him readied their guns. They could hear the squawk of the birds now.

'We are nearing the river island,' whispered the colonel, finger on his lips to signal silence. A beautiful bird, its plumage resplendent, flew up but the nawab let it go. Too beautiful, he said, and added that was a surkhab, a sheldrake. The river was getting noisier, for the mud island had divided the river into channels, and the flow grew louder and more rapid as they strained up the eastern strait. The colonel and the nawab now readied their guns at the shoulder, though they were still at a distance from the island.

All of a sudden, they saw the whole island rise up in front of them, as if some bird god had summoned the entire waterfowl kingdom to the skies. It was a shock for Sudhakar—a thousand water birds, *murghaab* and *kaaz*, geese, grebe and mallard, swamp hen and tern rising like some gigantic cloud, bird cloud, squawking and screaming and cackling during this winged lift-off. Many of the birds were wet. Light shimmered as it alighted on their backs only to slip off, as if it had glanced off shards of galvanised steel. All three of them were stunned by the scene, this vast latticework of wings moving ahead to the accompaniment of the cacophony of bird cries.

'They bring the north here every winter, isn't it?' asked the nawab rather philosophically.

'Yes, they must be wondering why they took the trouble to come here, flying a thousand miles, if they were to be chased out.' That was Sudhakar's contribution. A flock of waterfowl circled around and flew off on cue, their cries sounding a bit querulous, as if they were asking what kind of an island was this with guns on the lookout.

They were now alongside the island and the colonel asked if they would want to alight. Both Sudhakar and the nawab declined. They noticed a straw hut on the far side of the island and suddenly a man appeared on the scene. He was hunkering down and now he stood up. He was bearded and had a stick in his hand. Even from the distance he seemed to be in a poor state, more apparition than man.

The nawab shook his head. 'I don't think we will get many birds today.'

Why must you be pessimistic, chided the colonel.

The nawab did not reply.

'Who could that man be?' asked Sudhakar. He had pointed his camera at the man but thought he was too far away.

'A hobo probably. The down-and-outs choose peculiar places.'

The nawab agreed with the colonel. 'The man could be off his nut.'

Sudhakar kept talking about him, still wondering who he could be, why the birds had crowded the island despite him being there. Why on earth were they not frightened of him?

The birds had now settled on the banks, but they had seen the boat and were keeping an eye on it. Each time they were within gunshot, they flew away. Each time the nawab shook his head.

Meanwhile the beer bottles had been opened and the liquid poured into the glistening tankards bearing the insignia of the regiment. The nawab was having none of it, he never touched alcohol.

'With all this activity we won't get a thing,' the nawab remarked yet again. 'A month back, I came here on bullock cart and travelled along the bank. I shot twenty birds.'

Sudhakar was not having a bad day, though. His camera had kept clicking.

The river shimmered under the sun. They decided to circle the island now and return along the other bank. As they neared the straw hut they saw what they had so far been calling the apparition. He was wearing a sort of robe of cotton twill. It was dirty and old. His face was sun-blackened, the cheeks hollow and the beard shaggy. They observed his falter-walk as he moved towards the boat. Sudhakar couldn't resist his curiosity and said he would like to get on to the island. His pretence was that he would get a good shot with his camera. They all got down. The apparition moved towards them.

'Where are you from and why are you living on this island?' asked the colonel kindly.

'If one's needs are few, one can live anywhere he wants, sahib.'

Sudhakar was startled. He felt unreal, he didn't know why.

'But why here?' persisted the colonel. 'Why on this island with the birds?'

'The birds don't trouble me. I don't trouble them.'

'What is your name?'

'What has a name got to do with it, sahib? One lives with the river-wind and the river, with bird and fish, and with silence, with the seasons and the night.'

Sudhakar had stood rooted so far. Something touched a memory nerve, the gait, the voice. He staggered a bit and couldn't get the words out of his mouth. The nawab caught him by the arm, but he gently shook him off and advanced towards the birdman.

'Sukhdeo?' he said, looking intently at the man and advancing towards him, hope shining like two torchlights from his eyes.

The birdman's face lit up.

THE HIEROGLYPH CAVE

The cave of hieroglyphs dazzled me, frightened me, but it was not something I was going to confess to anyone. I had retreated. People get upset when faced with a circumstance beyond their comprehension.

I happened to tell a friend one evening that I intended to explore the suburbs of hieroglyphs.

He shook his head, unable to understand.

There must be something beyond sign and symbol, I told him.

What, he asked, rather befuddled.

I didn't feel like elaborating on this long enduring quest of mine, but about that later. There was also a cave from which I had drawn back, much like the leopard who had come to our island and retreated; about that too, later.

First one must talk of triumphs, not retreats.

When I invented the first letter of the alphabet, I was feted. Amphorae of olive oil and small jars of honey, corn by the bushel and sheaves of crackling golden wheat were placed at my doorstep. Who would have fancied when my stylus encrypted the first letter on wet clay that it was such a great feat? Spearing a charging boat was a much bigger thing than this squiggle, I would have thought. People compared it with the first dig that hit a metal seam in the dark hollow of a quarry. All they were looking for was stone for arrowheads, stone soft enough to be sharpened, yet strong enough to kill. Rumours said that they were looking for the stone which produced a spark when rubbed against another stone. And the fellows lit upon metal! No telling when people hit the jackpot. (Suddenly stone and flint shares fell through the floor in the arrow and spear-blade markets.)

Guys compared the first letter with Shyamak's discovery of fire. Pardon my arrogance, but all that the bugger had done was to hurl a piece of flint at a deer, miss it (fellow must have been cockeyed) and hit another stone. Fire leapt out. He became famous in Persian lore as the one who had 'invented' fire, if you please. I went on lecture tours telling people that in summer on the black continent, when dry savannah grass turns twig-hard and brittle, the sun starts fires which consume reed and scrub and runaway cattle. Herds of wildebeest get charred. So what was the big deal? But would anyone listen?

My discovery was no fluke. The first letter Aleph fell straight as lightning on poplar. Sound and design came to my mind in a single flash. The second letter came to me through cussedness, I admit. A parliament of brown baboons was making such a din on the treetops, that I followed the shepherdess as she herded her congress of sheep to the pastures. She looked more like someone from Arcadia, she was so beautiful. The sheep dutifully uttered 'ba' and the second letter was born.

Then letters tumbled over each other, swarming my mind. Words followed, words in fact started exploding like pigeons from a cornice. Bird-cries put in a demand for words—the kite's knife-edged keen, the nightjar's tut-tut, the raven's caw. The drum, flute, strings—they wanted separate words for distinct sounds, thought I was a word-bank! Became tough at times, but then I also wanted to be known as the inventor of words. You can't have ambition and not back it up by working your butt off. That's an axiom with me. See what that one letter, Aleph has done—belief, resolve, godhood itself flows from it. Altar, Allah, altitude, altazimuth, alcohol, the alexandrine line, imagine what that one letter has spawned. None can challenge the oneness and loneliness of the solitary Aleph.

What was important though was that the boat of language had sailed from our island.

But what about that retreat of mine, so far not adulterated by words? I went into the cave of hieroglyphs, though warned by philosophers and those who pass off for the cognoscenti. Don't go there, they said. Your limited mind will be baffled. Limited? Me? I strode in. A symbol or two I could make out, but the rest was elusive, and each sign had something sacred coming down seemingly from centuries to back it up with. Shadows here suddenly started painting away as if they held a piece of charcoal between their fingers. The cave walls started speaking—I heard sounds which were not sounds, music which was not music as I knew it, but something more mysterious, more numinous, something that recalled a harmony that had existed for ages among man and trees and animals and grasses, and some spirit that passed like a breeze through grass and scrub, a spirit that had kept watch over dust and desert, wind and rain, over how the stars moved. I suddenly felt I was not fit to be here, this was hallowed ground.

☛

One is entering the sphere of legend here. There were two legends—the first of course about the clouded leopard swimming across to the island from the mainland. What made him do it? What impelled him, asked the minister of forests, a favourite in the government of the Universal Sister. The second legend was the leopard's return.

When he appeared on the island he didn't look drenched. As he emerged on the beach, some islanders swear that not a drop trickled off his silken back. Others swear that when he shook the water from his pelt, he drenched half the beach. Still others said that when he shook the salt off his flanks, his spots fell off! He didn't bother with the crowd that gaped at him, but quietly made his way up the hill to the cavern known for its terrifying beauty. People started following him thinking it was a god in the big cat's avatar. Forest tribes believe that divinity descends on leopards and tigers at times. No one knows what actually happened except that the clouded leopard had retreated.

They heard a guttural snort as he padded into the cavern. The leopard's pupils turned green in the light reflected from the jade walls of the grotto. Filaments of light struck his eyes. The shaman of the forest tribes speculated that the leopard thanked his stars that the reflections that were ricocheting off the walls were spawned by half-light, or he would have been blinded.

The leopard realised he was not up to it, there's only so much beauty you can confront. Others had survived, but he, lithe of limb and muscle, knew this was not for him. The clouded leopard retreated from the caverns of clouded jade, and went his way.

THE AMPHIBIOUS TRAIN

Children, you are gazing at my scanty beard which looks like a mandarin's now, the kind you must have seen in Chinese paintings. And I notice you sometimes stare at my cap, which I wear only to hide my bald pate. You, of course, have been told that I am no mandarin. I sometimes notice your elders looking a bit disdainfully at me. The other day a mother tugged her daughter back as she wanted to run into my arms, a kid of six perhaps, in her pigtails and her blue uniform. That was Deepa, was it? Thanks. I didn't know her name. Names now disappear from the mind like clouds from the sky when there's a wind. I felt sorry for the child and sorrier for the mother.

Sorry, am I speaking too loudly? But it's high tide and I can hear hardly anything except the sea. The sea makes a lot of noise, thinks we are all deaf—thank you for the laughter.

Yes, and your mothers must have told you I am no mandarin but a retired boat owner. Yet when you sell your boats, you are still sailing or rowing or commanding someone to adjust the sail, or if you are in a motor boat, you're telling the helmsman to be careful with that wheel now that you are nearing rock or shoal. Your dreams rock you side to side, your nights are still rolling or lurching on the waters. Man, you are on land! But trouble is, you can't speak to yourself in sleep, and even if you did, you can't listen. Listening is always tougher than speaking. So at nights, my dreams toss me about. That's what owning a boat does to you, children, and I owned several—three motor boats, three sailboats, a dinghy.

Why did I sell them? Firstly did I? I'll come to that, but to start with, let me get you kids some corncobs. Hey Monsieur Hawker, Seignior Khomchawala, bring the lot here! I'll buy them all. You want a lollipop? You get a lollipop. Yes, and smear some lime and salt on the cobs. Can I carry on with the story now?

Boats ply from mainland to islands or the other way around, that's what people tell you. That's what even sea winds will tell you. My boats had dreams—easy, easy. I know boats can't dream. Well, mine could. They always thought they were sailing from island to island; they were a bit deluded, but then you wouldn't know what that means. If you're going north and think you're going south, that'd be a delusion. Yes, you're right, if you are swimming in water and think you are swimming on land, I mean walking on land, that would also be a delusion.

My boats refused to leave for the mainland! But they had no problem plying the seas as long as you avoided that huge mass of land. How did they know it was the mainland, you ask? Child, they can smell it, every boat has a nose fitted in its prow.

So I lived on the island known as Santa Xavier and plied my boats eastwards to other bits of land surrounded by the seas. I can't blame my poor boats for wanting to dock there. Who wouldn't want to be moored to the island? White sand, not a scrap of paper or plastic on the beach, it was a great place. We had lovely trees—laburnum, flamboyants, bottle brushes—and the streets were cobblestoned. No dirt on the roads, all the garbage in the bins, not a crumb outside, and not a dry leaf anywhere.

All was fine till one day the president, Richard Gonsalvez Kutty, announced he was bringing a train to the island. We shook our heads in disbelief. No one wanted a train on the island, was the fellow crazy? We walked, we biked or we went by bus. He must have been drunk when he announced it over the radio, we thought, and got on with our lives.

One day, we heard the hoot of a steamship. That's a cargo boat, said Mukundan, who could zero in on a boat merely hearing foghorn or hoot. People came to the docks to watch it. But it was too big to risk the shallows of our harbour, and stayed away while all kinds of boats sped towards it. What do you think they started unloading? Any guesses, children? Rail tracks, that's right, you get an extra ice stick and a corncob for that.

This set the cat among the pigeons. We scratched our heads. Was it a mainland bloody cat among island pigeons? We were dismayed to find it was our presidential cat among pigeons! Our island tongues wag like any other. Various theories started doing the rounds. The president had lost on the gaming tables at the casino, said the rumours. You know what a rumour is, children? It is an underground whisper that nobody can hear, yet everyone hears. That is a rumour, the most dangerous underground thing apart from earthquake tremors.

The president had to recover his losses somehow. 'He barking on makin' enough dough, baby, to buy an island for hisself,' hissed Mukundan. A cut on the tracks, a cut in the wages paid to the half-starved migrants, who had come packed like sardines in the hold of this cargo ship.

'Where food coming from?' asked a lascar called Krishnan. 'They think sea got enough fish to feed the scum?'

The prime minister, Vappala John, will set matters right, I told him.

'What can pri minister doo? Can make speech only, bloody fellow. Money count on gamming counter, how prez will go to casino, if no money in pocket? Tell, tell. Chillun, that's how he used to speak, this lascar Krishnan. Not rascal, lascar!'

Other rumours soon started floating. Sorry, sorry child, yes if rumours are underground how can they float? Very good question. I've no answer. Anyway this rumour said that the train was amphibious. We didn't know what that meant. Well, actually, it meant that the train could move over land and on water. How, we asked? Does the train have water skis? The rumour was spread by the president's men. Now people cheered the migrant labourers, cheered the laying of the track. Damn fools.

Like a paper boat a third rumour was set off. The train would cut pollution on the island. We lost our shirt, hearing that. We stoned the labourers, we threatened to set fire to the train if it ever came up, we stormed the parliament but were beaten back badly by the police. We asked Grotto Island's president to invade us and save us from this horrible president of ours.

How sad, but our movement and agitation broke into two groups. This is actually a mainland sickness, but it had travelled to the island. One group, which I followed, said we won't be able to breathe the air here, birds will die, fish will die, if the train comes.

The theory of the other group was frightening, devilish and sinister. What does it mean, you ask? Sinister means devilish. They were led by a man called Thomas. Children, he was a mystic, but don't ask me to define that word for you. Ask your dads. Thomas would play the flute and then say that so-and-so saint came and said such-and-such things to me. We wouldn't see the comings and goings of the saint. So we would ask, when did you meet the saint? The reply we would get is, 'I met him alright, could have been in my dream.' Questions were put to him regarding his dreams. 'My dreams are real. They have a ground to walk on, music and sound, each dream has a different voice.'

Now Thomas spread the rumour that the island itself was a dream. That Santa Xavier didn't really exist. If the train came to it, it would sort of solidify, become real.

Yes children, I agree it is very difficult to imagine an island on which people are living, and yet one that remains a dream.

But then, there were others who said at the first hoot of the steam engine the island would vanish, would turn into a dream.

More than the crosswinds of the rumours, real, blustery winds started encircling our island. The sea, which was a glassy blue till now, turned brown. Before a storm comes, wind and sea enter into a conspiracy. You know what that means? I see quite a few heads nodding—you brats are seeing too many of these Indian crime movies—all Indian movies are crime movies, aren't they?

The seagulls also conspired with wind and sea, they were the first to move to the island. Well, a storm was brewing. The cargo boat was on a jam as it bucked and reared against the walls of white foam and salt. I thought the boat was doing yogic asanas on the sea. The spars were snapping and the captain decided to lighten the ship; goods were thrown overboard including the rail tracks. You'd imagine they would go to the sea floor, but the waves were so strong, they washed them onto our island. Some were washed a few miles astern onto the Grotto Island. So there you have it. The train and track were amphibious. See!

And soon, children, all the rumours and contrary theories (we could almost call them prophecies) were proven right. The train ran on sea and land. And worst of all, the island, we learnt, was a dream. It just vanished. Obviously my ships too vanished in search of islands. They were damned if they were going to trade with the mainland.

I forgot to tell you, the only good thing that happened was that the wretched president, Richard Gonsalvez Kutty, also drowned with the island, the one who first tried to bring the railway in. But while the island vanished and didn't sink, that wretched Kutty sank.

☛

It was getting dark now and two worried young men in trainers and shorts asked the old man, 'Who exactly are you talking to, Father?'

'I was talking to the children. Oh, where have they disappeared?'

'These are dogs, Dad, not kids. The children must have left after you gave them corncobs. It's so late, we were frantic. Mama sent us out to look for you. It was the corncob vendor who told us where to find you.'

'Oh, Seignior Khomchawala?'

'Yes, if that's what you choose to call him. And Dad, why are you after that Kutty fellow, he gave us a fair price for your boats! Do you hold a grudge against him?'

The other brother added, 'He was just the president of the boat union here. You've made him the president of an island. Father? You hold his post against him too?'

'How do you know I said these things, if you just found me?'

'We were standing behind you, Dad, for the last ten minutes, and heard you. And what is this about an island—about a dream turning into an island, or island turning into dream? You seem to be inventing a new story every day?'

'Well, son, what is wrong with inventing a new story every day?'

AFTERWORD

Since I am still savouring the afterglow of my second novel published a few months ago, the old chestnut about shorter and longer fiction needs to be got out of the way. And I can do no better than the Latin American novelist Carlos Fuentes, who described a short story as a boat and the novel as an ocean liner.

I have been on this boat now for over thirty years, sometimes through choppy waters, unsure how to round off a story or where the written word should intervene in something you are conjuring up. Thought process is gossamer while the first written word could be likened to a hammer nailing something into the ground.

As is only too well known, the short story has developed an aesthetic of its own over the last few decades, especially in the West. A long rumination or the depiction of a mood can pass off for a short story today. Event and plot have taken a back seat. There need not be any finality at the end. Writer and protagonist can get into a tram or bus and go home leaving the story hanging in the air. Let's say a boy and a girl want to elope. They discuss, plan their exit, express their feelings and regrets at what they will be leaving behind, and both go home leaving the physical elopement for the morrow. End of story. What happens to them the next day is not considered important.

In India we have more or less stuck to a plot. As I look back at the stories I wrote in the seventies and later, plot and event got into the foreground. In half the stories, irony played its part as an underground voice. And now and then one hitched a story to a historical event, the way one hangs a painting on a nail. But history, or to put it less hyperbolically, historical events, were not so much a prop as an igniter of the imagination. For instance the story 'The Day of the Winter Solstice' is about a recurring dream that has troubled the Brahmin Govardhan, who lives on the banks of the Kali Nadi. In the dream he sees his wife Janaki weeping over a corpse, displaying all the insignia of widowhood. The story is pegged to a battle in District Fatehgarh during the Mutiny of 1857. Govardhan thinks that the dream foretells his death. The untrained horse which eventually broke the defiant square of the Telungas (mutineers or rebel sepoys) was actually dredged from history. It would be impossible for me to swear whether the thought of the mutiny in Fatehgarh struck me first or the idea of the dream.

'When Gandhi Came to Gorakhpur' is obviously a take-off on the burning of Manchester cloth. Though 'the word Gandhi had come like a double beat upon this kettledrum country', obviously the treatment couldn't have been straightforward anti-British sloganeering. The ironies in life, especially in the political field, need to be brought out.

There are stories here which I wouldn't have written today. For instance I went hammer and tongs in a story against triple talaq, the way it is practised under the Sharia Law. The story was more relevant in the nineties. I reluctantly redrafted a page or two. I firmly believe that all work must defend itself. The written word, especially the printed word, knows by instinct that it has to defend itself against posterity.

I have always enjoyed setting the scene first, house, locality, light, termite-eaten logs and tethered cows in the backyard of a small time Gorakhpur lawyer; or a carpet being beaten by the flat owner living above in the story 'Also on You be Peace.'

I enjoy slapstick, and am not embarrassed by the admission.

Some stories have an anecdote behind them. Once I browsed through a book of French stories. One was on a Trojan horse, who comes into a bar and calls for a drink. Trust the French to write such surreal stuff. Why can't I write a story about a Trojan horse, I thought? The treacherous metaphor was handed to me on a platter. How would a Trojan horse fare in the horse market after the fall of Troy? And the seed of the story was sown. In fact the story is metaphor made flesh. Since one had been brought up on Greek and Persian myth, why not let the fancy roam in these environs?

The story 'Bars' too has an anecdote to it. I got a notice of the publication of a volume of stories related to sectarianism. I knew the editor, a fine scholar and writer, Dr Rakhshanda Jalil, and asked her if I could write a story on the subject. She replied the book was in the press. I still wrote the story, in less than a week, drawing upon my experience as a Member of the National Commission for Minorities. It reflects the current reality we live with.

Now I write for entertainment, leaving it to the reader to fish for metaphor and moral and meaning.

I am certainly happy with my recent stories, all written in two months starting April 2016. Firstly they are first person narratives from women. Secondly I have moved away from the rural outback to the city. Some of the narratives are about moods, or a fragrance floating up from a just-watered garden. The shifts are not premeditated. They happen. My next novel is going to be a first person narrative from a daughter of a communist. When I wrote my first novel on the times and voyages of Vasco da Gama, a poetry volume, *The Map-Maker* came flowing out side-stream. Happens.

ACKNOWLEDGEMENTS

'The Russian Story' and 'Love Across the Salt Desert' first appeared in *Sword & Abyss* (Har Anand Publishers).

'The Day of the Winter Solstice,' 'When Gandhi Came to Gorakhpur,' 'Crossroads,' 'The Bride Returns,' 'And on you also be Peace' and 'High Pastures' appeared in *Minister for Permanent Unrest and Other Stories* (Ravi Dayal publishers).

'A House in Ranikhet' 'Trojan Horse' and 'Story of the Seminar' appeared in *A House in Ranikhet* (Rupa & Co).

'Bird Island,' 'The Hieroglyphic Cave' and 'Amphibious Train' appeared in *Islands* (Tranquebar Westland).

'Bars' appeared in the *Pigeons of the Domes* edited by Dr Rakhshanda Jalil (Niyogi Books).

'The Long Night of the Bhikshu' was first published in the *India Quarterly.*

The author wishes to place on record his thanks to the above publishers for the use of the stories in the current volume.